THE TRUTH REVEALED

BOOK 2 OF THE TRUTH KILLS TRILOGY

SEAN LA'MONT

THE TRUTH REVEALED

This book is a work of fiction. Although it contains incidental references to actual people and places, these references are used to lend the fiction a realistic setting. All other names, characters, places and incidents are the product of the author's imagination. Any resemblance to actual persons living or dead, events, or locales is entirely coincidental.

Cover Design and Art by Sean La'Mont
Book editing by Chell Morrow

For my mother.

Acknowledgments

I must thank my extremely supportive family members, my friends, and faithful supporters, for the Sean La'Mont, that I am today.

To my teachers, Mr. Donald Robinson (dance), Mrs. Gwen Fairley (economics), Mrs. Wright (dance), Ms. Pat Ponich (drama), Mr. Oley Kittleson (drama), Mr. Roger Slater (social studies), Mr. Roberts (art) and the Principal, Mrs. Florence Johnson of San Diego School of Creative and Performing Arts, thank you for nurturing my talents and creativity.

To "Giff", Rick, Jonathan, Jeff, the Owners, and entire staff at AAA Digital Imaging; you have taken my art to another level. I would not have a business without you.

To Tippy, Karimah, and Allen, I must give you thanks. Your framing transforms my art into masterpieces.

To IKONS magazine (Andranae Byer), Meak Productions (Miko Evans), Persona Online Magazine (Sean Robinson) and TRUTH magazine (Uriah Bell),

Thank you all for your unwavering support, encouragement, and National exposure.

To my baby sister, Kimberly, thank you for your input, helping me create the wickedly fascinating character, Yvonne Jones.

To Denise Henderson, thank you for introducing me to the brilliant, spoken-word Artist, Marvell Wilson. A special thanks to Mr. Wilson for your written contribution. After reading "THE TRUTH KILLS", you were able to channel Isaiah's emotions with your GOD-given talent. It is an honor, to have your poem; 'ISAIAH'S PLEA' open THE TRUTH REVEALED.

I want to give special thanks, to my Aunt Laura, for your editing skills, and keeping the story real. Thank you for sharing your vast knowledge on everything, and your exceptional gift of paying attention to detail.

Thank you, GOD, for this life that you have given to me. I am exactly where you put me. Though the trials and tribulations are driving me to the brink of destruction, I know you will not give more than I can bear.

THE TRUTH REVEALED

ISAIAH'S PLEA

WRITTEN BY MARVELL WILSON

Before me now
lies my greatest fear
...an unfamiliar emotion
I must pioneer
To come to some terms
as to how I now feel
about a notion and a vision
that is no longer real
Engaged by a challenge
that in itself, is unique
extremely difficult to fathom
...even more so to critique
I must gather my wits
in an effort to survive

this fiction...a contradiction
poised to eat my spirit alive
...wound and bound by events
not of my own want or will
where a lie
encouraged a life
that only the truth had power to kill
I must address the mathematics
of this solitary lie
all additions
have become subtractions,
with no chance to multiply
I must skillfully weigh and measure
the sum of confusion
I feel inside
Where a solution
to the problem
leaves no choice
but to divide
Yet, despite all the clever science
there's still one factor to contend
a potion attached
to the quotient
of feelings of love
that linger within
So in light of this present equation,

I'll most humbly
request of you
through e-mail, twitter, or telepathy,
share some advice on what
I should do

ONE

Nicole stood in front of KNB Art Gallery, located in Rock Crest, a bustling, upper middle-class, outdoor, shopping mall.

She read one of the many large posters, neatly arranged on the storefront glass of the unopened gallery.

"Please join us, for the Grand Opening of KNB Art Gallery, Friday November 4th at 7:00 pm, Complimentary champagne and wine. Receive a FREE greeting card and envelope, while supplies last." There are several examples of her framed charcoal drawings, artistically displayed on the poster. In bold pink letters read, www.knbartgallery.com.

Evening attire preferred.

She unlocked the front door, and hurriedly walked inside, careful to lock the door behind herself. She turned on the lights and quickly walked into her small office, located in the rear of the nearly completed, 1400 square foot gallery. After deactivating the security system, she placed her purse and keys on her desk.

She removed her full-length, leather coat and draped it over the back of the office chair. She straightened out her oversized black sweater, that hung over her tight, stretch black jeans and low-heeled black boots.

She casually sauntered back into the front of the carpeted gallery. She shut her eyes and took a deep breath, pretending to be a customer entering KNB for the first time. Nicole intended to name the art gallery after herself but decided to use her deceased sister's initials as a dedication. Kyla Nicole Bennett was her younger sister. Kyla was her first supporter and biggest fan, who encouraged her artistic ability.

She opened her eyes and to the right of the front door, sat her favorite drawing of Rashidi, Isaiah's son. The drawing was exquisitely framed and matted in rich mahogany wood, set on a deluxe chrome tripod.

The gallery windows were covered with heavy maroon curtains in order to conceal the gallery contents.

On the right wall, in the front of the gallery, hung the framed autographed celebrity section. Several of the drawings had a SOLD card, in the upper right corner. There were various celebrities and personalities, she and Isaiah had the opportunity to share her art with.

She could distinctly remember meeting some of the people they admired, where they met them, and the celebrities' reaction to her work. She remembered how proudly Isaiah would present her art to them.

She missed him.

Even though they lived in the same house, they were a thousand miles apart. They had returned home to Atlanta for two weeks, and they rarely spoke to each other. She kept herself busy with the gallery, and assumed he did the same at the garages.

After the autographed celebrity section of the wall, she continued to gaze at the other famous celebrities, ranging from recording artist to deceased political figures. Each piece of framed art, had the title and price in the lower right corner. On the back wall of the gallery, in large pink and black letters read: CUSTOM PORTRAITS AND FRAMING. A small section of various frames and matting options are on display, with a large pricing chart.

She decided to feature three portraits she drew of Michelle's two sons and her baby sister Kyla's portrait, in the center.

This area also included her in gallery art studio. It also included a check-out stand, complete with a cash register, credit card reader, cordless phone, and sturdy leather and wood barstools. She provided extra barstools for her customers to sit in.

Her art studio station included a large, adjustable drafting table. Her rolling workstation was stocked with pencils, charcoal pencils, blending stumps, cans of acrylic spray, and plenty of clean hand towels.

To the left of the back wall, was the door that led into her small business office. The left wall, near the back of the gallery, hung her tasteful nude and semi-nude portraits. This section also included her "SEASHELLS" series, male and female images on the beach. The left wall, near the front of the gallery, ended with religious portraits. A varied section of female and male ballet dancers. Portraits of couples, in the park, and on the beach, or in a passionate embrace. On the left side of the front door, sat two large, rotating, greeting card display racks.

In the center of the sizeable gallery, sat two large, light-gray, art bins, placed back-to-back. The art bins held large-sized art prints, individually, and profession-ally packaged in plastic sleeves, with a price sticker on each piece, in the upper right corner.

As she glanced around the gallery, she felt incredibly blessed. It was hard for her to believe that she created all 92 pieces that hung in her gallery. Eventually, she planned to include other artist's work, once she established the gallery.

Thank you, Lord.

Her impossible dream had finally become a reality. She knew she owed it all to Isaiah. He had become the most influential person in regard to guiding her art career. Isaiah submitted the application to the first art show Nicole had ever participated in. It felt strange not to have him right by her side, because she really valued his opinion.

She decided to keep herself busy.

Nicole walked up to her drafting table, where she had previously begun working on a new piece of a beautiful blond, blue-eyed toddler, dressing her Barbie doll. She would title the new piece, 'Future Designer'. This is the fourth drawing in her future series.

The first drawing is of Rashidi, Isaiah's son, in a three-piece suit titled, 'Future President'. The second drawing in the series is an adorable African American toddler, listening to her puppy's heartbeat, titled, 'Future Doctor'. Malik Jr., Michelle's oldest son, dressed in his Halloween football costume titled, 'Future MVP'. She would unveil her "Future" series after the gallery's grand opening.

As she sat in front of her drafting table, thoughts of her dissolving relationship with Isaiah flooded her mind.

Nicole heard banging on the front glass door. She walked up and peered out the side of the maroon curtains that covered the glass door.

It was Michelle, her best friend.

She unlocked the door and let her in. "Hey Mrs. Reed, welcome to KNB Art Gallery." she hugged Michelle.

"Good morning, Mrs. Mathis." Michelle responded, cheerfully.

"No, it's Miss Bennett." Nicole knew that she would never be Mrs. Isaiah Mathis. "What are you doing here? I'm surprised to see you," she forced herself to smile.

"Hey Honey, what's wrong with you? You sound like somebody died."

"Michelle... I screwed up. Our relationship is over."

"What do you mean, it's over? You and Isaiah?"

"Yes, it's really over. These last two weeks have been hell. He won't even look at me. I really hurt him. It is all my fault. I wanted to tell him the truth about me in the beginning. But when I first laid eyes on Isaiah, something inside my soul told me that he was the one. He was the man I dreamed about my entire life. He was so perfect...there was no way I would have jeopardized a potential relationship with him. I had no other choice but to withhold the truth about my past. I don't think Isaiah will ever forgive me. I'm not worthy of Isaiah."

"Girl, bye, you need to stop that negative thinking. Ok, yes, I agree with you, maybe you should have told him, but don't beat yourself up about it now. He can either accept it or reject it, it's that simple. I have something to show you."

"Shouldn't you be on your way to work?" Nicole asked.

"I was. I stopped to get my morning coffee, and saw the headlines on the morning paper. You need to see this." She handed Nicole a portion of the newspaper. "Read the headline of the sports page."

Nicole read the headline aloud. "Former Professional Football Superstar, set to open his fourth celebrity hotspot in Atlanta...oh my God." She gasped.

"How about that? Is this a coincidence or what? He *just* might be the one behind those manila envelopes. The newspaper says that he will be in Atlanta this weekend. Your gallery opens this weekend. What's up with that?"

"He might not be responsible for the envelopes. I'm sure he's forgotten all about me." Nicole hoped.

Michelle could see the headline of the sports page really bothered Nicole.

"Please don't be fooled by these double-d's, and all this junk in my trunk, I can box!" Michelle started shadow boxing in her office attire like Muhammad Ali, jabbing and sparring, which made Nicole laugh.

"What would BB want with me? He could have anyone he wants, with his conceited, arrogant ass. Besides, he's married." Nicole explained.

"Trust me sister, you ain't got nothing to worry about, I got you. You really think it's over, you and Isaiah?" Michelle felt bad for her. She knew how much Nicole loved Isaiah.

"We hardly see each other. He's been working longer hours between the two garages."

"You mean, Isaiah's Complete Car Care." Michelle corrected, using the name Nicole created.

"And I have been so busy with the gallery grand-opening this weekend. By the time we both get home, we go straight to bed."

"That's good, right?"

"He is still sleeping in the guest bedroom."

"So, when was the last time the two of you had hot, butt-naked sex?"

"Once, while we were in San Diego."

"Damn, that's not good. Come give me a hug." Michelle hugged her softly. "I'm sorry, I can't imagine being without sex for two weeks. After I get off work tonight, you want to go to one of them nasty, adult, sex shops? You can buy a big pulsating, vibrating, latex friend. Honey, they even have one you can attach on the shower wall, and back that thang up. Girl, I would kill myself with no meat in my diet."

"Don't tempt me."

"I'm kidding; Isaiah needs more time. Your past was a hard pill for him to swallow, especially when the truth about your past came from an escort magazine, and not from you. I know Isaiah, and Isaiah is not the type of man to beat around the bush. He obviously still has feelings for you, or he would have left a long time ago."

"But it's his house too, we split the down payment. The house belongs to both of us."

"No matter what happens, you still got me. Isaiah will come around. Trust me."

"Has he said anything to Malik?" Nicole asked.

"Malik hasn't said anything to me. Speaking of my husband, I had to help him adjust his attitude towards you."

"I don't understand. What attitude?"

"He developed an attitude towards you. It started the day we picked you and Isaiah up from the airport. You remember, you told me about your past, being transgendered and then we dropped you both off at home. I was mad as hell with Malik for withholding such important information about my best friend. You are family and I had a right to know. I'm his wife; there is nothing he shouldn't tell me. Then I questioned him about how he treated you at the airport. I noticed the distant handshake and asked him why he developed negative feelings towards you."

"You're right; I noticed that too. I figured that Isaiah told him the truth about me. Normally, Malik hugs me and kisses me on the cheek."

"Exactly. He had the nerve to tell me that he didn't want you around the boys anymore. Like what you and Isaiah are going through affects our relationship with you."

"Are you serious?" Nicole asked. That really hurt her feelings; she loved their children like her own.

"Don't trip, I lit his ass up. I reminded him of all the great things you have done for us, especially for the boys. Your creative ass constructed both of the boys, letter and number books. You personally taught both of our sons how to read and write. Now they both love to read and we owe that all to you." Nicole smiled. "Before you and Isaiah decided to open the gallery, I reminded him of all the times you offered us childcare at no cost. How many babysitters educate your children?"

"Thank you, Michelle." Nicole smiled.

"Oh no honey, I'm not done. He couldn't count the times you two took care of the kids so we could take weekend getaways. Isaiah didn't watch the boys before you came. You are the best friend I could have ever hoped for. Your past has nothing to do with the woman you are today. To be honest, your past was shocking, but it never changed the way I feel about you."

"Thank you for having my back, Michelle." Nicole hugged her.

"No. Thank you for being a true friend, not only to me, but to my family. The next time you see Malik, you will notice that his attitude is back to normal. And as far as you and Isaiah go, just be patient and hold on."

"I have no choice. I don't want anyone except Isaiah. I have never felt love for anyone the way I feel for him. It's so hard to see him and not touch him."

"Damn girl, I couldn't even imagine. You know what? You just remain focused on the gallery and everything else will fall into place. What time is it? Oooh girl, bye, let me get my butt to work."

She unlocked the door for Michelle.

"Keep this door locked, you know that crazy quarterback is coming to town. I hope I ain't got to whip nobody's ass this weekend." Michelle said aloud as she exited the gallery.

"Thank you, Michelle, have a good day at work. I love you, sister."

"I love you, too." Michelle turned around placing her hand on Nicole's shoulder. "And by the way, every time I come in here, it looks more beautiful. Nicole, I am so proud of you."

"Thank you, Michelle."

"I promise I will stay on Malik to talk to Isaiah."

"Thank you."

"And if you see that crazy quarterback, you know I got your back."

"I know." Nicole laughed. "What are you doing for lunch? Maybe, we could have lunch together, I really need someone to talk to."

"Of course, I'll see you around noon. I love you, Nicole."

"I love you too, Bye, Michelle." She locked the gallery door.

Two

"Complete Car Care, Isaiah speaking." He answered.

"What up, dog?"

"What up, Malik? I can't complain."

"What's up with you and Nicole? Ya'll back together yet?"

"Naw man, same shit. We basically live under the same roof."

"So, what's up with that? You still have love for her, right?"

"Malik, she was my best friend. I trusted and confided in that woman. She was my soul mate. I loved Nicole, more than I loved my son's mother. Nicole knew everything about me, and I didn't know shit about her. Everything she told me was lies, the lies about her parents, and their supposed accident, in which they both died. The lie about BB, the quarterback, and the most important lie, was that she was not born a woman. Could I ever trust her again?"

"Damn, that's some real shit."

"Sometimes, I just wanna snatch her sexy-ass up and make love to her until she can't walk no more. And then at other times, looking at her makes my stomach turn. I'm moving out, man."

"What about Complete Car Care, doesn't Nicole handle all the accounting. What about the gallery? Can you imagine life without her?"

"I have no choice Malik, I can't do it."

"Well, it's a done deal. If that's what you need to do, I got your back. Speaking of the quarterback, did you read the sports page this morning?"

"I haven't got to it yet? What's up?"

"Brock Bass is opening another B.B's Sports Bar here."

"What?!" Isaiah stood up in his office. "Here in Atlanta?" He didn't know how to respond. He didn't know why, but the sudden possibility of Nicole reconnecting with BB, seriously bothered him.

"Yes, Sir. The paper said he's due in town this weekend, out of nowhere, and the same weekend as Nicole's Gallery grand opening. What's up with that? She might have been telling the truth about her relationship with Brock. You might want to warn Nicole."

"Good looking out, I'll call her now."

"Go ahead, holla at me later."

"Good looking out, Malik." Isaiah hung up the phone.

I can't just call her, he pondered, *I ain't said shit to her in weeks*. He began to pace back and forth inside his office. He decided to read the sports section. After reading the article, Isaiah knew that he had to call her. He thought about Brock. *What if she was telling the truth about her relationship with him? If that motherfucker goes near her, I'll kill him*. He searched thru his cell phone contacts and found the gallery number. He dialed.

After two rings, Nicole answered the gallery phone. "Good morning, KNB Art Gallery."

"Good morning, how are you?"

"Isaiah?"

"Hey, how you doing?"

"I'm fine, thank you. How are you?" She asked, surprised to receive a call from him.

"I'm aw'ight." He missed talking with her. "I called to see if you read the sports section of today's newspaper?"

"I've seen it; I haven't had a chance to read it yet. Michelle brought it to me. She just left."

"You aw'ight?" He asked.

She felt herself longing for him. *He still cares.* She didn't know what to say.

He heard the uncomfortable silence. He wanted to tell her that he missed talking to her and that he still loved her. He wasn't sure that it was the truth or his need for sexual release. "So, uh, do you think he will come looking for you?" Isaiah asked her.

"I doubt it; it has been almost two years. Why would he care? Like I told Michelle, he could have any one he wants, why would he want me?"

"Why wouldn't he want you?" *Damn, what the hell did I say that for?* "Hey, I gotta go. I guess I'll see you at the house, have a good day."

"Thank you. You too." She heard him hang up the phone.

What the hell did I say that for? I know I have feelings for her, so why can't I accept her for who she is? I wish I didn't know the truth, he thought to himself.

"Hey, Isaiah, Chuck wants to holler at you!" Ray-Ray, one of the mechanics in the garage yelled. Isaiah walked out of his office, to the customer service counter.

"Hey Chuck, what's up? How business?"

Chuck Wilson was also a mechanic who had a service garage in the neighborhood.

Isaiah walked around the counter as they shook hands.

They had become friends.

"I'm trying to put your black ass out of business," Chuck said as he wrapped his arm around Isaiah, and they both laughed. "What's going on boy? How you been? Came in here twice, a couple of weeks ago, where you been?"

"Nicole and I went to Cali; she had some family issues."

They both walked into the service garage.

"How did you like California?" Chuck asked.

"Cali's tight; reminds me of home in Florida."

"How is Nicole doing? I haven't seen her in the garage for awhile. I can spot her car a mile away."

"You have my garage under surveillance or something?" Isaiah laughed.

"Hell yeah, it ain't every day you get to interact with a woman as sweet and fine as Nicole." He laughed. "You a lucky brotha."

"You know her art gallery opens this weekend."

"I know. We got an invitation. That's all my old lady Pauline is talking about. I'm telling you that girl is going to make it as an artist. God blessed her with too much talent. The portrait she drew of Pauline and me is still hanging over the fireplace in the living room. And the other one she did of our children and grand-children is hanging in the family room. Pauline is going to kill one of them children, trying to steal our artwork," he laughed. "We thought the gallery invita-tion, was a wedding invitation. When ya'll getting married, again?"

"We decided to hold it off for now. We want to get the gallery off the ground first."

"Boy, you got cold feet?" Chuck asked.

"Something like that." Isaiah answered.

"Don't hold it off too long, someone else might come and snatch her up."

"You right, man." Isaiah responded, realizing that Chuck might be telling the truth.

"You know what? I just had an epiphany. You and I could merge, and form Chuck and Isaiah's Complete Car Care. How does that sound?" Chuck laughed.

"Man, if you don't get your old ass outta here." They laughed.

Harry Jenkins, another mechanic in the garage joined the conversation.

"What up, Chuck?" Harry asked.

"Hey, Harry," turning his attention back to Isaiah. "You just keep referring your customers to the best."

"You just take your old butt back to your old Sanford and Son garage." Isaiah laughed.

"You know, I had a Mercedes last week. It was an older one though, transmission tore up," Chuck said.

"I ain't mad at you." Isaiah replied.

"Boy, you should have seen the woman driving it, she was fine as hell! She had to be a stripper, or a prostitute, because she had on a little tight red dress and a pair of red high-heeled stilettos. Boy, you could see everything."

"I'm sure you gave her one hell of a deal." Isaiah and the guys laughed.

"You damn right, I fixed her transmission for free. She tasted so good; I didn't brush my teeth for three days. We did it right there in my office. Boy, when I got finished going downtown, looked like I dipped my face and neck in a bucket of cooking oil." They all start laughing again. "I bet you all the fine women be coming up in here."

"Hell no, all the fine women go to the yum-yum man's garage." Isaiah said and they all laughed again.

"Man, forget you Isaiah; don't try to act like you don't creep with the ladies." He elbowed him. "Come on now, you can keep it real with me; I'm old enough to be your daddy."

"Not once." Isaiah stated.

"With a woman as fine as Nicole, I believe you. Hey

man, I gotta roll. I'll roll back thru later. I'm out!" Chuck replied.

"Alright, Mr. Wilson." Harry laughed.

Chuck saluted them as he walked out of the garage.

"That old man is crazy," Isaiah said to Harry. "I'm going back to my office."

Chuck Wilson reminded Isaiah of how his father might have been. His father was a mechanic who died rapidly from prostate cancer when Isaiah was thirteen years old. His mother was devastated. With costly hospital bills, and funeral, their insurance money, and their savings accounts were depleted. They could no longer afford to live in the house his father provided. They moved to a lower income neighborhood in Florida. His sickly, grieving mother was forced to become head of household. She found a job in housekeeping at a hotel; barely earning enough income to provide for herself and young son. She did her best and when Isaiah started attending high school, he began to hustle on the side, behind her back to help her make ends meet.

"Isaiah, the phone, man." Harry yelled.

Isaiah hastily answered the phone in his office.

"This is Isaiah, may I help you?"

"What's up, Dad?"

"Rashidi," he exclaimed as he beamed with pride.

The sound of his son's voice made Isaiah's heart smile. "How you doing, Son?"

"Good." Rashidi smiled into the receiver. "Dad, I think I died and went to heaven, junior high is crazy cool. All the girls are dimes here, all of them." Isaiah laughed. "I never really noticed them before, and now I want one."

"Hold on son, does your mother know how you feel?" He was glad that his son felt that he could talk to him about anything.

"You know I can't talk to Mom about girls. I'm her baby."

"You want to talk about it? I have some free time."

"That's why I called you. How is Nicole? Isn't the grand opening this weekend?"

"She's fine, what's up?"

"Would it be ok if I came down for the weekend?"

"Boy, you know you are always welcome here. I wish you would come and live here, permanently."

"You know I want that too, but mom acts like she can't live without me. Maybe you can convince her that I'm becoming a young man, and I need to be with you."

"You know your momma ain't trying to hear that."

"That's because you try to convince her over the telephone. I bet you could persuade her in person. Would it be ok if mom came with me?"

"What?!" Isaiah hadn't seen Yvonne in person, for years and he wanted to keep it that way. Their only communication had been via telephone, when Rashidi was in his care. He always kept their conversations short.

"How else are you going to convince her that I need to be with you, my real father? She wants to come to the gallery grand opening." Rashidi explained.

Isaiah would do anything to have his son in his life on a permanent basis. If I have to suffer for a couple of days, dealing with Yvonne again, I could do that, he thought. "Yeah, I guess that's cool." What am I going to tell Nicole? Isaiah thought to himself.

"Do you think Nicole would be upset? Mom really wants to meet her. I talk about her all the time. Mom loves the drawing she did of me. Should I call Nicole, first?"

"Hey, that's a good idea. You know Nicole can't say no to you, and I'm sure she would love to have you here at the grand opening. You need the number?"

"No, she gave it to me already. I will call you right back."

"Do that. Love you, son."

"Back at you, I mean... I love you, too, Dad. Bye."

THREE

Nicole read the newspaper article...

Brock Bass, former Professional Football Superstar, Football Channel, and Sports Channel host plans to open his fourth BB's Sports Bar and Grill in Atlanta. His other locations and Casino include Los Angeles, Las Vegas and New York. His newest location will be on Peachtree St. in Buckhead.

The former two-time MVP of the Los Angeles Quakes, recently divorced his wife, Ashley Meredith Huntington-Bass. They settled out of court for an undisclosed amount. They had no children in their six year marriage.

Prior to his marriage to Ms. Huntington, Mr. Bass had been known as a ladies' man, romantically linked to many of Hollywood's leading ladies such as Meagan

Fields, Amanda La'Fleur and Award-winning actress, Caroline Connors. Mr. Bass is arriving in Atlanta this week to finalize negotiations. He recently purchased an upscale condominium development in the Buckhead community. The 41 year-old, sports celebrity and entrepreneur, will be hosting several black-tie events throughout Atlanta in the upcoming weeks.

She felt her heart beating in her throat. *Does he know that I live here? This is no mere coincidence; he's coming to find me,* Nicole thought to herself as the gallery phone rang.

"KNB Art Gallery, can I help you?" She answered.

"Hi, Nicole."

"Is this Rashidi? I was just admiring your portrait, thinking about you. I wish you could be here for the grand opening."

"That is why I'm calling, Mom said I could come."

"Really?! When are you getting here? Does your father know?"

"I just talked with him; he said it was cool."

"So when do you get here?" Nicole asked.

"There's something I want to ask you first." Rashidi replied.

"Whatever it is, yes."

"Mom wants to come too; she really wants to meet

you. She loves your artwork. She brags to all her friends about my portrait that you drew."

Nicole didn't know what to say. "What did your father say?"

"He's cool with it. We wanted to make sure it was cool with you. We are trying to convince my mother that I should live in Atlanta with you and Dad."

No wonder Isaiah said yes, he wants Rashidi here with him, Nicole rationalized. "I don't see a problem, of course she can come."

"Thank you, Nicole, I can't wait to see you and dad, and for you to meet my mom. Have you done any new artwork?"

"I have created several new pieces. I can't wait to get your opinion. You're my favorite art critic."

"Thank you. See you Thursday night. Mom is letting me skip school on Friday for this."

"It is for a good reason, we only have one grand opening. Bye, Rashidi, see you Thursday." She hung up the phone.

That is only two days away, she panicked. She had to get the house ready for guests. *What if this woman doesn't like me? What if I don't like her? Why all of a sudden does she want to come to Atlanta?* She immediately wanted to call Michelle at work, but she knew that she would see her for lunch.

―――――

Nicole decided to bring up the subject of Rashidi's mother, Yvonne visiting, over lunch with Michelle at the popular local cafeteria. "You know Rashidi is coming to Atlanta this weekend for the gallery opening."

"I love me some Rashidi. When does he get here?" Michelle asked.

"They arrive Thursday night." Nicole responded.

"They? Who is they?"

"His mother is coming with him."

"What! Girl are you crazy? Malik said Isaiah can't stand that woman. You never let your man's ex into your home, never."

"I already said it was ok."

"Well, call her back and say hell no."

"I can't, Isaiah said it was ok, too."

"I know Isaiah hates that woman, why is he allowing her come here?"

"He is going to try and persuade Yvonne to allow Rashidi to live here, permanently."

"Hell, he could do that over the phone. She doesn't need to be in your house. You know Yvonne got married while Isaiah was locked up for taking care of her funky butt. Is she bringing her husband?"

"Rashidi didn't mention his stepfather, just him and her."

"She is the main reason Isaiah got locked up. Malik told me Isaiah got deeper in the drug game, trying to provide for her selfish, pregnant ass. She had to have the best of everything, and she never contributed anything. Malik said she was never satisfied. Isaiah gave that girl everything. He even made provisions to take care of her while he was locked up. Can you believe that? I hate women like her, self-centered bitch." Michelle fumed.

"Hopefully, she doesn't want Isaiah back, he belongs to me."

"You better watch that shady, gold-digger, especially around Isaiah. Make her get a hotel room."

"I trust Isaiah, even though we are having problems. He wouldn't do that to me."

"She would, I don't like her, and I never met her. You better than me, she wouldn't be in my house."

"But I really enjoy Rashidi when he is here with us. His presence always makes the house feel complete. I live out my fantasy as a mother and a wife. We are a real family, and they look so cute together."

"You right girl, do it for Rashidi. And if sister gets out of line, you let me know. She ain't never met me, so I can beat that ass. Besides you have bigger issues to worry about like Isaiah and that crazy quarterback. Speaking of that crazy quarterback, how did ya'll meet again?"

"I met Brock Bass when I was a transsexual escort/call girl."

"You mean a prostitute." Michelle laughed.

"Pretty much. My parents threw me out the house when I was sixteen years old. And when you're young, with no place to go, without a formal education, guess where you end up, on the streets. I was fortunate enough to meet Peppa when I did or I could have ended up a street walker, hooked on drugs or even worse. That's when I became an escort, trying to earn the money for my reassignment surgery. My escort name was Sabrina." Nicole recollected with Michelle, the first time she met Brock Bass, through the Southern California Connections escort magazine...

Nicole's thoughts trailed off...

Three Years Ago...

"Hello?" She answered the house phone.

"Hello, is this TS (transsexual) Sabrina?" He asked.

"Yes, this is she. How are you?"

"I'm fine, thank you and how are you?"

"I'm fine, thank you for asking."

"You are the young lady in this advertisement?"

"Yes Sir, that's me." She responded, cheerfully.

"You sound exquisite. Sabrina, if you look anything like your picture, I'm in serious trouble."

"I've been told I look a lot better in person."

"Oh really? I'll be the judge of that."

"And what is your name?"

"You can call me, Billy."

"Ok, Billy, how can I help you?" She asked.

"I'm visiting San Diego from L.A. I guess I'm looking for a little companionship, maybe even a tour guide."

"Are you visiting San Diego for business or pleasure?"

"Considering I called you, I assume a little of both. Are you available now, for an outcall?"

"Yes, I am available now, but I only accept in-calls."

"What part of San Diego are you in?"

"I live in the Mission Hills, Hillcrest area. Are you familiar with San Diego?"

"I'll get there. How far are you from downtown San Diego?"

"Approximately, fifteen minutes away, Fifth Avenue will bring you straight to me."

"And you're sure, that you're the girl in the picture?"

"Yes," she laughed. "You already asked me that."

"Sometimes these ads are misleading. You meet a girl,

and she looks nothing like her advertisement picture, or she has posted someone else's picture."

"Billy, I promise you that I will look exactly like my picture, or better. I assume you have done this before, been with a girl from the ads?"

"Yes, I have seen real women from the ads. But when I saw your pictures, you totally captured my attention with your natural beauty. As I read your ad, it stated that you were TS. I have never been with a woman like you. I'm going to be frank with you Sabrina, I have always been curious about transsexuals, but never acted upon it. I absolutely love women. I've never had a desire or attraction to other men. Your ad pictures are quite unbelievable. Are you really a transsexual?"

"Yes, I am, is that a problem?" She asked, becoming defensive.

"I'm looking at your pictures now, and I can't believe you're a transsexual. Even your voice sounds so feminine."

"Yes Sir, seeing is believing."

"I like your attitude, Sabrina; you sound like an amazing girl."

"You sound very nice yourself, Billy."

"I can be there in less than an hour. What's your address?"

"First, I need to ask you a couple of questions, if you don't mind."

"Go for it."

"What do you like to do, sexually speaking?"

"I'm an all-American male, oral works, if you're good, and of course, penetration, me on top of you, period. Pardon me for being so blunt."

"It's ok, it comes with the job. I just want to inform you that I am very selective about who I let penetrate me."

"Are you serious, in your profession?"

"I say that because some of the men I date are extremely well-endowed. And I refuse to allow any man to ruin me. What did you give the last girl you were with?"

"What do you mean, what did I give her?"

"The last girl you saw from the ads, what did you bring her?"

"Oh, I see, I gave her $500.00 for the hour. Is that ok?"

"You want to get together in an hour?"

"However long it takes to arrive at your destination. I don't believe you gave me your address."

"Once you're in my area, call me from 5th and University."

"Sabrina, I am extremely discreet. We will be alone, correct?"

"Of course."

"And one more thing, if I look at you and see any masculinity, I will walk out. I told you earlier that I am not into men. I am willing to compensate you for your time. Is that, ok?"

"That sounds fair."

"Good, I'm on the way."

"Goodbye, Billy."

He arrived at her door exactly one hour later. He knocked on the door.

She answered the door wearing a soft pink push-up bra with the matching panties and a floor-length pink chiffon robe. On her feet she wore pink, high-heeled mules with pink feathers over the toes. She applied a minimal amount of make-up, exactly like her picture in the advertisement. Her naturally curly, shoulder-length hair is French twisted up the back of her head, held in place with a large, decorative rhinestone comb. Large elegant, rhinestone, clip-on earrings hung from her earlobes with wide, rhinestone bracelets on both wrists.

When she opened the front door to the apartment, Brock/Billy was speechless.

Her expensive, fragrant perfume overwhelmed his nostrils.

"Are you just going to stand there?" She asked seductively, smiling as she stared into his sunglasses.

He removed his sunglasses to get a better view.

Nicole was shocked at how handsome Billy was, minus the excessive facial hair, and ponytail, protruding from under his baseball cap. He was tall, with a husky, athletic build.

She assumed he was in his mid-thirties.

His rugged good looks and solid frame, coupled with his slight arrogance, made him even more appealing. His skin was tanned to perfection. He walked in.

She closed and locked the door behind him.

"You smell delicious." He said, impressed with her poise and beauty.

"So do you. Please have a seat." She motioned him to the large, black leather sofa.

He was casually dressed in surfer shorts, tank top and sandals. He carried himself as though he was wearing an Armani suit.

She could tell he was the type of man accustomed to having things his way.

He wore an obvious Rolex watch and the indentation of a non-existent wedding band. She assumed he was married.

"This is very nice," he said carefully surveying the immaculately decorated living room. He walked around and looked at the art and furnishings. "You have a beautiful home, very nice. I love this drawing, this one of the ballerina."

"Thank you, I drew that."

"Are you serious?" He walked up closely to the framed artwork, to survey her work. "You drew this? The details are amazing."

"Yes sir. My bedroom is filled with my drawings. I can show you if you like."

"Interesting... I would really like to see that."

"Ok, can I offer you something to drink? Beer, wine, mixed-drink, or bottled water?"

"Water, please." Nicole saw that Billy was quite comfortable entering new surroundings for the first time.

He sat on the leather couch.

She walked into the kitchen and came back with two bottled waters. As she walked towards him, her robe opened, billowing behind her to reveal her long, sexy legs.

"You are absolutely stunning. I guess seeing, really is believing. You are truly unbelievable. I cannot tell you weren't born a woman."

"Well, thank you. You are quite handsome yourself." She sat close to him, in order for him to feel her soft skin. "Here you go." She handed him the water.

He placed it un-opened on the coffee table.

"Thank you."

"You're welcome. Will you open this one up for me please?"

He took the bottled water from her and opened it, then handed it back to her.

"Thank you," she smiled at him.

He liked her mouth. He found it strange that he wanted to kiss her, knowing that she was a man.

"Would you mind if I made myself more comfortable?" He asked.

"Not at all, please go ahead. Make yourself at home."

He stood up, removed his baseball cap, ponytailed wig, and removable facial hair.

"I must wear a disguise when I leave the house. I'm an extremely private person. You can never be too careful." Billy/Brock sat back down.

"Wow." Nicole initially thought Billy was ruggedly handsome, but without his disguise, he was gorgeous. She wondered why he would pay for sex; women would have sex with him for free. He could be the spokesperson for success. "You look awfully familiar. You remind me of a..."

"I used to play."

"Play what?"

"Football."

"Really? What position?"

"Quarterback." She knew that she recognized him; she just couldn't remember his name.

"Oh my gosh, you're..."

He kissed her.

She felt the passion that exuded from his lips. She pulled away from him, trying to regain control of the situation. "Uhm, would you like to go get more comfortable, in my bedroom?" She stood up.

"Sure," he stood up.

She could see his massive erection, tenting the front of his shorts. "Are we here alone?"

"Yes, but I have a roommate."

"Is she like you?"

"You mean a transsexual? Yes."

"I told you earlier, I insisted that we must be alone."

"We are alone, I have my own room. The door has a lock. You will not see or hear my roommate unless you want to." She smiled.

"There is someone else here. Can we go back to my hotel room? I'm staying at the Omni Hotel, have you heard of it?"

"Yes, in Horton Plaza."

"I'd feel much more comfortable there."

"I'm sorry; I never do outcalls, unless we've had previous interactions."

Billy reached into his back pocket and retrieved his platinum, diamond-encrusted, money clip.

"Here you go, let's get this out of the way." He handed her $1000.00 dollars. "Will that be enough?"

"I don't know."

"That donation also includes you being my tour guide. We don't even have to have sex unless you want to. We got a deal?"

"I don't know."

He pulled her close to him.

"I promise I won't harm you. I'll even meet your roommate; show her my driver's license, whatever it takes. There is something about you that I find intriguing."

"Uh...ok, can I go get my roommate?" She asked, smiling softly at him.

"Sure."

They are standing face to face.

"What's your last name? Or should I just say Billy?"

"Everyone calls me B.B." She knew that she had seen him before. His name was Brock Bass, the celebrity football player. She could hardly contain her excitement.

"Ok, I'll be right back; I'm going to get her."

"Take your time." He responded. Nicole walked out of the living room and rushed into Peppa's bedroom.

Peppa was standing behind her bedroom door, awaiting confirmation that her date was safe.

"Guess who is in the living room?" She whispered to Peppa.

"Who?"

"Brock Bass," she whispered.

"B.B, the white football player?"

"Yes, ma'am."

Peppa wasn't surprised. The majority of Nicole's clients were Caucasian.

"He gave me this." She handed the money to Peppa.

"You better work." Peppa smiled, counting ten new, crisp, one hundred dollar bills.

"He wants to meet you. He wants to take me with him, back to his hotel room. He says he needs a tour guide. We don't even have to have sex; he claims that he finds me intriguing."

"You are intriguing. You go back out there; I will be right out."

"Ok." Nicole sauntered back into the living room.

Brock is looking at the pictures on the fireplace mantel. He picked up the gold-framed, picture of a little girl as he saw Nicole walking towards him. He held the picture out for her to see.

"Who is she? She looks just like you."

"That is my baby sister."

"I thought it was you, when you were a little girl." He placed the picture back onto the fireplace mantel. He reached between her legs and firmly grabbed a hold of her genitals. "I guess you really are transsexual."

"Keep holding on to it, I promise it will grow." She smiled, provocatively.

He released her abruptly. "I'm not into that. I had to verify that you are in fact, a transsexual. You move, feel, sound, and act, like a true biological female."

"I hear that all the time. I paid very close attention to my mother, growing up."

"I'm serious, you are really unbelievable. I bet guys hit on you all the time and have no clue that you are a transsexual. I'm curious to see how people will react to you, once were in public."

"You're right; guys never question my true sexuality."

"That's because you're fucking gorgeous."

"Well, thank you, Billy."

"Please, call me B.B."

"I will." He leaned in to kiss her.

Suddenly Peppa entered the room wearing a black teddy with a matching floor-length black robe. She wore a blunt cut, asymmetrical wig, and black, high-heeled stilettos.

"Hello, how are you?" Peppa said, extending her hand, elegantly.

"B.B, this is Peppa, and Peppa, this is B.B." Nicole introduced them.

"I'm fine, thank you for asking. How are you, Peppa?" They shook hands.

"I'm fine, thank you for asking, Mr. Bass."

"Please, call me B.B."

"I will. I see you fancy my Sabrina."

"I do. I am interested in becoming more familiar with Sabrina on a personal level. I would like her to act as my personal tour guide. Give me the grand tour of San Diego." He looked directly at Nicole. "If that's ok with you?"

"It would be an honor to be your tour guide." Sabrina/Nicole smiled at him.

"How long do you plan to keep her?" Peppa asked.

"A couple of hours, three at the most. Is that, ok?" Brock answered.

"That's fine. What hotel are you staying in, while you're in San Diego?"

"I am registered at the Omni Hotel in Horton Plaza. The name I am using is Dennis Meyers, in the penthouse suite." Brock answered.

Peppa made a mental note to verify this information.

"Brock, I'm sorry...BB, I hold you responsible for her

wellbeing. I want her brought back the same way you take her from here. Understand?"

Brock felt like a school kid on his first date. "Yes, Peppa." He laughed as he turned to face Nicole. "Are you going to wear that Sabrina?"

"Oh no," she laughed. "I'm sorry; I'll just take a minute." She dashed out of the living room.

"Please have a seat B.B," Peppa motioned him to the leather couch.

"I'll stand, if you don't mind. You have a beautiful home. Did you decorate yourself?" He asked, admiring the elegant furnishings throughout the living and dining room area.

Peppa sat on the matching love seat. She noticed the wig, the baseball cap, and artificial facial hair on her coffee table. He must wear a disguise in public to protect his identity, she thought. "I did, thank you."

"I love this charcoal drawing of the ballerina. Where did you get it?" He pretended that he couldn't read the signature.

"Sabrina drew that. She's an incredible artist."

"She said that she stores her drawings in her room. May I see some of her other artwork?"

"Sure, let me go get them." Peppa exited the room and returned with Nicole's large black portfolio.

She set the oversized portfolio on the side of the

couch. Then she removed her coffee table decorations and placed them on the kitchen table. She placed the portfolio on the coffee table and opened it for Brock.

He was sincerely impressed in the way she captured her subjects with her realistic charcoal drawings. The details in the eyes, allowed the viewer to see into the subject's soul. "She is really talented. Did she go to school for this?" Brock asked.

"No Sir, natural, God-given talent."

"Has she shown these to anyone?"

"No Sir, she doesn't think she's good enough. I have tried to convince her to go to art school. She has other immediate goals in sight. So, what brings you to sunny, San Diego?"

"I needed a break from LA. Have you ever been to Los Angeles, Peppa?" He turned the page of the large portfolio.

"I've been there to visit. I thought it was nice, wouldn't want to live there."

"She's never been to art school? This is absolutely unbelievable." He said, referring to Nicole's art, then redirected his conversation to Peppa. "Why is that? What's wrong with LA?"

"I'm originally from Chicago, born and raised. Then I lived in New York for five years and then in Hawaii for two years. Then I decided I wanted to see

California. LA is too congested. I fell in love with San Diego, and I have been here ever since. I guess I was ready to settle down. I may change my mind someday. Who knows?"

Brock felt completely at ease talking with Peppa. "Sounds good to me." He said, focused on the art.

"San Diego is a beautiful city. Have you been here before?" Peppa asked.

"Yes. I have been here several times before. San Diego is very romantic. I believe the last time we stayed at the Hotel Del Coronado."

Who is we? Peppa assumed he was married. Brock turned the page of the portfolio.

"Yes, I've been there. Did you know that is where they filmed the movie, 'Some Like It Hot' with Marilyn Monroe, Jack Lemmon, and Tony Curtis?"

"I knew that; they had memorabilia from the movie." He is stuck on a drawing of Audrey Hepburn. "I have to have this one. Does she sell these?"

"Not really, she gives them away."

"We can't let her do that. You don't ever give away an original."

"I've tried to tell her that, maybe you can convince her. What part of San Diego is Sabrina showing you today?"

"I don't know, we haven't decided yet. How long

have you known Sabrina?" He was curious as he closed the portfolio.

"I have known her since she was sixteen. I knew we were going to be close the very first day that I met her."

"Really? What a coincidence, I've had the same premonition."

"I adopted her. Older transsexuals tend to do that with the younger girls."

"I see," Brock smiled. "Why doesn't Sabrina pursue a career as an artist? She's obviously has the talent."

"That's a great question, you should ask her."

Nicole sauntered into the room. She was dressed in comfortable, faded-blue, stretched-denim, Capri-shorts, and white spandex, spaghetti-strapped, tank-top with a white, padded, push-up bra. The bra made her small bosom appear much larger. She also wore white strappy sandals and pink sunglasses. Her pink backpack containing a sexy outfit, heels, and a small cosmetic bag, with contraceptives and lube hung on her right arm.

She pulled the decorative comb from her thick, naturally curly hair as it cascaded over her shoulders. She handed the comb to Peppa.

"Ready?" She smiled at Brock.

"You look great." Brock smiled as he began to put back on his disguise. He then walked over to Nicole.

Peppa smiled with pride.

"I'll carry that for you." He said to Nicole as she handed him the backpack. "A gifted artist should only use her hands to create. You are an amazing artist."

"Thank you." She smiled at him. She turned around and hugged Peppa. "Bye, Peppa. I will see you later, ok?"

"Ok, have fun." Peppa responded. Peppa escorted them to the front door.

"Really nice talking with you, Peppa. I hope to see you again." He shook her hand.

"Likewise. Take good care of Sabrina."

"I will," he assured Peppa. She opened the door for them and locked it behind them.

They begin to descend the staircase that lead to the parking lot in front of the building.

"Does Peppa think that she is your mother?" Brock asked.

"She is my mother. I have known Peppa ever since I was sixteen years old."

"Why? What happened to your real parents?"

"It's a long story."

"Are you from San Diego?"

"Yes Sir, born and raised."

"The perfect tour guide."

"Yes, I am." He deactivated the car alarm for his rented SUV.

He opened the door for her.

She climbed inside as he closed the door behind her. "Wow, you have a beautiful truck."

He slid into the driver's seat. "This is not my truck, it's a rental. I am very private when it comes to my personal life, which is why I wear the disguise. Put on your seatbelt. Your mother would kill me if anything happened to you." He laughed.

"What can I show you first?" She asked, enthusiastically as she settled into her seat.

"You tell me." BB said. He enjoyed looking at her.

"Have you ever been to La Jolla?"

"I don't believe I have been there before."

"Well today is your lucky day. Take a right at the corner." They drove to the cove in La Jolla; past the elegant, world-famous boutiques and restaurants.

They exited the truck and walked to the shore.

"This view is spectacular."

The landscape and natural rock formations confirmed that GOD was the only one who could have created such a view.

"We don't have coves this beautiful in Los Angeles. Or maybe it's your presence that allows me to fully appreciate its beauty."

He smiled at her. "Are there any good restaurants around here that you would recommend?" Brock found Nicole fascinating; he couldn't keep his eyes off of her.

He found himself waiting for her to show him a sign that she was in fact born male. Everything about her, her mannerisms, her speech and natural body structure exuded female.

"Are you kidding, La Jolla has some of the finest dining in the world. I'm afraid that we aren't dressed for fine dining. But I know another great spot for sight-seeing and tourists. Do you like Mexican food?"

"I enjoy all types of food."

They jumped back into the truck and drove to Old Town.

They went into and were seated in Las Margaritas.

"I can't believe that you don't have a boyfriend." Brock commented, sipping on a beer.

"I have met lots of guys outside my line of work. In the beginning, we are fine. As soon as I tell them the truth about me, they won't accept me, or our relationship becomes strictly sexual. I refuse to live my life as a woman with male genitalia. Once I have my surgery, I will never tell anyone about my past."

"How long have you been an escort?"

"Too long."

"So why do you do it?"

"I have no choice. I hate being an escort; but I also hate that certain part of my anatomy, even more.

Escorting offers me a chance to generate the type of cash necessary to have reconstructive surgery."

"What if I told you that I really like you and I accept you for who you are? Would you believe me?"

"I guess I would believe you, but that wouldn't change anything. I can't truly be happy with myself, until I am a complete, functional woman. I refuse to live my life incomplete."

"You're a great artist. Why don't you pursue an art career? There are several pieces in your portfolio, that I must own."

"That has always been a dream of mine. But my first priority is my surgery. You can have any of the drawings that you want. I will draw some more."

"Please, don't ever give your art away. You have a gift. People would pay top dollar for a Sabrina original. You need to start a business and sell your artwork. You need to learn how to form, manage, and operate your business. You need to go to art school. Promise me that you will not give away any more art."

She laughed. "I promise." She had never met a total stranger who had taken such interest in her art.

The waitress brought their food to the table. They began to eat.

———

"He was so nice to me. He treated me just like a princess." Nicole told Peppa, after she returned home from her date with Brock.

"Did he take you shopping?"

"We went to a jewelry store in Old Town. He had me try on a $4000.00 tennis bracelet."

Peppa's eyes lit up with anticipation.

"He asked me did I want it. I told him, no."

"Are you crazy?! Brock is a trick. You take whatever they give you."

"Not Brock. Peppa, I can't explain it. It's like I have known BB, since forever. He was so different, like he was proud to be with me. He had already given me a thousand dollars. What more could I ask for?"

"I'm sure he asked for sex. What did you have to do?"

"He left that decision up to me. I explained to him that sex is just a job to me. I do it because I have to, not because I want to. He asked me did I want to have sex with him. Yes, I did. Since he already paid me, I gave him oral sex and he exploded into the condom. I offered him some of his money back."

"What?!" Peppa, hollered.

"Listen, he said I could keep the money. Maybe, next time."

"You honestly think that he would come back to see you?"

"He might, and even if he doesn't come back, I really had a good time. Besides, he's married anyway."

———

"Well, he obviously called back." Michelle eagerly added, thoroughly engaged in Nicole's recollection of life with Brock Bass.

"A few weeks later, Brock did call back. Peppa answered the phone." Nicole told Michelle, as she relived her memories...

———

"Hello?" Peppa answered.

"Hello, how are you? This is Pepper, right?" He asked.

"Yes, this is Peppa. Who is this?"

"B.B, you probably don't remember me. I'm a friend of Sabrina's. Is she available?"

"Yes, I remember you. How are you, B.B?"

"I'm great, thank you."

"Hold on, let me go get her."

"Sure."

Peppa covered the receiver with her hand. "Sabrina, the phone."

Nicole picked up the phone in her bedroom.

"Hello?" She answered.

"Hello, Stranger."

"Who is this?"

"It's B.B. You've forgotten me, already?"

"Hi B.B, how are you?" Brock could hear the excitement in her voice. Nicole wanted to tell him that she watched his show a few times on the Sports channel.

"I'm doing very well, thank you. For some strange reason, I can't stop thinking about you."

"Are you serious?" She smiled. "I thought about you, too."

"I was wondering, are you available this weekend?"

"Yes, which day?"

"The entire weekend. I'm sure you won't be able to service any of your other clients. I'm prepared to compensate you for your losses. What's your average take on weekends?"

"I don't know, it varies."

"How about $3500.00, plus expenses, does that sound fair?"

"Yes, I guess."

"Ok, $4000.00 and not a penny more."

"I'll take it," She laughed. Nicole couldn't believe it.

"A couple of questions first; do you have a valid driver's license?"

"No, I have state-issued identification. I don't drive."

"How old are you?"

"I'm 25, why?"

"You're 25 years old, and you don't know how to operate a motor vehicle?"

"Why should I? Everything I need is convenient to where I live. I don't need a car. We use a cab if we have to."

"What is the name that appears on your ID?"

"What? Why do you need to know that?"

"Trust me, ok? I need to know your name exactly, as it appears on your ID."

"B.B, that is very personal. I can't tell you that."

"I know your real name is not Sabrina. I'm positive your biological parents did not address as Sabrina as a young child, please, trust me."

Nicole is hesitant. "Brock, I don't know."

"Sabrina, I don't have all day."

"OK, it's Jonathan. Jonathan Lamont Bennett. I'm in the process of legally changing my name. Happy now?"

"Jonathan Lamont?" Brock laughed. How do you spell that?"

"J-o-n-a-t-h-a-n-L-a-m-o-n-t-B-e-n-n-e-t-t."

"In about an hour, I want you to go to the nearest Western Union and pick up the money. The sender's name is Dennis Meyers. I will wire you half of the money as a down payment. You will receive the remainder, after you leave. Do we have a deal?"

"Yes, but..."

"I will call you back with your flight information."

"Flight information?" Nicole asked, suddenly alarmed.

"You're coming to Las Vegas."

"Las Vegas? BB, I hate to fly."

"Why?"

"Why, what? I hate to fly."

"Once you board the plane, you have a nice, chilled glass of champagne, maybe two."

"I'm going to need more than champagne; do they offer crack or heroin?"

Brock laughed. "It's not that bad. It's only a 45 minute flight, once you're in the air."

"B.B, I can't do it, I'm serious."

"Trust me, I would never ask you to do anything that would harm you."

"I believe you, it's the plane that I don't trust."

Brock laughed again. "Flying is safer than driving."

"Who told you that lie? People survive auto accidents. I have never heard of anyone surviving a plane crash."

"Will you please come to Las Vegas?"

"I guess, but you're going to pay extra for this."

"Not a problem. Oh, one more thing, my personal assistant, Dennis Meyers, will be there to greet you in the Las Vegas airport. I will wait in the limousine. While we are together publicly, Dennis will act as your boyfriend."

"What?"

"Sabrina, not only am I a sports celebrity; I also happen to be a very married man."

"I clocked the T."

"What?"

"I mean, I noticed."

"Well anyway, in case I'm recognized, I can't afford the bad publicity. Understand?"

"Yes, I understand." Reality reared its ugly head. I'm the rented whore, and he's the generous trick. I will be so glad when this part of my life comes to an end, Nicole thought solemnly.

"Good. People take pictures of you that you aren't even aware of, and that's the last thing I need my wife to see."

Brock wondered how much he could trust Sabrina. He heard some of the horror stories that his fellow colleagues had to endure; prostitutes blackmailing them, demanding more money, or threatening to go public with their private affairs. Brock dated several call girls and escorts, in every major city. He made it a rule never to see the same girl twice, no matter how good she was.

He learned this rule from experience. He became romantically involved with a young black female escort in Los Angeles. He wanted more than sex with her. They would often spend time together in public, with Brock usually in sunglasses and a baseball cap. Someone must have recognized him and took their picture. The very next day, it appeared in the gossip magazines. His wife was furious. Not only was he cheating, but she was African-American.

He will never forget his wife's promise. 'Next time you fuck a nigger, I will fuck you in court.' Brock discovered at an early age, that he was attracted to African-American women. His father, originally from Texas, discouraged his feelings, and informed him that it was merely a fetish. A relationship, with a black woman publicly, would jeopardize his future, outside of football.

His father also insisted that he marry Ashley Meredith Huntington, a wealthy socialite.

"Back to what I was saying; I need for you act as though Dennis is your boyfriend. That includes hugging and holding hands. He will accompany us, when ever we're in public."

"Does he know what I am?" Nicole knew she had to keep it business with Brock. No matter how much she liked him.

"You're a woman, at least to me you are. And that is all Dennis needs to know. We have done this type of arrangement before. He will never question your sexuality."

———

The flight in first class was relatively smooth with a minimal amount of turbulence.

Dennis Meyers was the perfect gentlemen. He was tall, thin, and somewhat attractive, with a terrific sense of humor. He appeared to be in his late twenties. Dennis made Nicole feel at ease in an awkward situation.

They stood at the front desk of the five-star hotel, awaiting their hotel room keys.

"Watch this," Dennis whispered into Nicole's ear. Dennis began to kiss Nicole on her neck and fondle her buttocks.

Brock was not in disguise, taking a picture with ardent fans. When he noticed them publicly making out, Brock became infuriated. He excused himself from his fans, and confronted Dennis and Nicole.

"What the hell is going on?" Brock whispered angrily to them.

Dennis and Nicole started laughing.

"Fuck off, Dennis. Let's get the hell out of here." Brock wrapped his arm around both of them, as they headed for the elevators up to their rooms, followed by the bellhops with their luggage.

"So you think Dennis is funny?" Brock asked Nicole, once inside the elevator.

"Hilarious." Nicole laughed.

They exited the elevator, to their adjoining suites.

Brock entered his room alone, while Dennis and Nicole entered their room. Dennis tipped the bell boy, as he exited the room.

Brock walked into their room, through the adjoining suite door.

"This is gorgeous," Nicole/Sabrina said, as she admired the room.

Brock took her by the hand, and escorted her to his room. Dennis followed him with her luggage. "I knew you would appreciate our accommodations." Brock smiled at her. Dennis placed her luggage on the side of the enormous bed. She laid her purse onto the bed.

"I'm going to settle in my room. Good night, see you both in the morning." Dennis said, walking back into his room, closing the door.

"Finally, I've got you alone." He kissed her softly on the neck and ears. "You taste so good." He walked her over to the immaculate, king-sized bed and he sat on the edge. He pulled Nicole towards himself. He hugged her around the waist resting his head against her flat stomach. She wrapped her arms around his neck. He looked up into her face. She smiled softly at him. He reached for her dress straps and lowered the top of her dress to her waist. He removed her bra and admired her small, supple breasts. He started to suck on them. "I want you." He lowered her dress to the carpet as she stepped out of it. "Nothing is going to pop out at me, is it?" He asked her.

"No, it's pretty secure," she laughed.

He kissed her stomach. He stood up, slowly. He kissed her gently on the mouth.

She unbuttoned his shirt, opened it, and pushed it back over his broad shoulders. She delicately sucked on his neck, working her way down to his chest. She focused on his left nipple, using just enough teeth to stimulate his nipple erect.

He moaned quietly.

She then repeatedly flicked his nipple with the tip of her tongue. She looked up at him.

His eyes were closed.

"You like that?"

He moaned louder.

Nicole knew she had control over him, as she reached into her purse for a condom. She ran her tongue down the center of his hairless stomach.

His erection tenting the front of his designer suit pants. She sat on the edge of the bed, as she sucked on his navel, while unbuckling his pants. After she unbuttoned and unzipped him, she lowered his slacks to the floor.

His thick, rigid penis, straining to be released from his silk boxer shorts.

She opened the condom and discarded the wrapper. She maneuvered the crotch of his underwear, so that his penis and testicles protruded from the opening. She lavished his testicles with her saliva, stroking them gently with her mouth as though they were his penis.

"Yes, oh yes. Mmmm." Brock was engulfed in sheer ecstasy.

She placed the condom on her lips and slipped it on Brock's hard cock. She took Brock all the way down her throat, as he threw his head back.

He grabbed her by her hair and used her mouth. He continually pummeled her throat with his sizeable penis. Brock exploded into the condom as Nicole milked every drop.

Then she kissed his hairy, beefy thighs.

"Come here." He said, as he assisted her to her feet.

He held her face with both of his massive hands and kissed her tenderly in the mouth. "Thank you."

"My pleasure," She smiled.

"I beg to differ." He stepped out of his slacks and collapsed onto the bed. "I believe that was the best blow job I have ever experienced."

"I bet you say that to all the girls," Nicole/Sabrina laughed.

"Trust me; I've experienced more blow jobs, than I care to remember. So when I say that you were the best, I mean it."

"Well, thank you, I'll take that as a compliment." She found the bathroom in the enormous suite, and returned with a warm, soapy, hand towel, and large, fluffy, white towel. She removed the used condom, cleaned his genitals, and dried him off.

She sat next to him on the bed. "So what are we going to do now?" She asked him, excitedly.

"I'm exhausted. I've had a long day. We had meetings, business proposals, and a late dinner. I sincerely apologize. My wallet is in the back pocket of my slacks. Get some money from it, go downstairs and gamble. Don't forget to use Dennis's room key."

"What if I want to stay here in the room and order room service?"

"Make sure you order room service from Dennis's room." Brock instructed.

"I give great massages." She removed his boxer shorts and socks. She started to rub his feet.

"Mmmm."

"Roll over, please." Brock rolled over, naked and lying face down on the bed.

She reached inside her purse and retrieved a bottle of lotion. She straddled him, sitting on his bottom. She put a liberal amount of lotion into her hands, and started massaging his shoulder blades. By the time she reached his lower back, she could hear him snoring softly.

———

The next morning, Nicole is awakened from noise coming from the large bathroom. She felt for Brock in the bed, as he emerged from the rest room, dressed in a flattering, pinstriped, dark-gray, Armani suit.

"Good morning," Brock said cheerfully.

"Good morning. Don't you look handsome?" She rose up in the bed, holding up the comforter to conceal her small breasts.

"Thank you." He strutted around the room like a peacock. "You like?"

"You look so handsome and debonair. What time is it?"

"9:15, I have a very important meeting this morning, with some very influential people."

"On a Saturday?"

"In the business world, a Saturday is just as good as Monday. The meeting is at ten. I should return no later than two. Make sure you are dressed and ready to go, when I return. If all goes well, I will show you the newest location of BB's Sports Grill and Sports Betting Casino. There's a few hundred dollars on the nightstand, in case you want to go downstairs and gamble."

"Thank you. Good luck, with your very important business meeting." Brock leaned over the bed and kissed her on the forehead.

"Thank you for being here with me to share such a momentous occasion. And I especially want to thank you for last night."

"You're welcome. Can I interest you in a quickie?" She offered.

Brock laughed. "Why don't we wait until this evening?"

"I'm ready, when you are." She smiled, sexily.

"I'll see you when I return. Make sure you get out of this room and have some fun. And don't forget to use the right room key." He opened the door into the adjoining room to Dennis.

"I won't." She said as Brock exited the room. Nicole stretched out and yawned. She decided to call Peppa. She used her cell phone, instead of the hotel phone.

"Hello?" Peppa answered, groggily.

"Hi Peppa, it's me."

"Where are you?"

"We're staying in the Bellagio. Brock's suite is bigger than our whole two-bedroom apartment."

"Damn. Did he penetrate you?"

"No, I gave him oral sex. I did that trick you taught me with the condom, worked like a charm."

"Good, so when will you be returning home?"

"Sunday night, I think."

"You missed a lot of calls. I turned the ones I could."

"How did you do?" Nicole asked.

"A little over nine hundred." Peppa answered.

"Good. You can have $1000.00 dollars of the money Brock wired me."

"You're almost there."

"I know. Another $12,000 and I will have enough to pay for my surgery."

"You keep dating Brock and he will pay for it."

"He is so good to me."

"He better be. Where is he now?"

"He had an important business meeting this morning. He's planning to open another sports bar here."

"So what are you going to do while he's gone?"

"I guess, I'm going to go downstairs and play the slots, after I have some breakfast."

"Well, call me later, and tell me what's going on. I'm going back to sleep. Thank you, for checking in."

"I love you. Bye."

"Bye, baby." Nicole showered, dressed and went downstairs for breakfast.

After the breakfast buffet, and turning down offers from several admirers, she played the slot machines. She then returned to the room, changed clothes, and put on her make-up.

She turned on the television and waited for Brock and Dennis.

Brock sauntered into the room at 3:27 pm. He threw his suit coat across the made up bed.

"You're late, Mr. Punctual." Nicole said to Brock.

"Who knew that it would be so time consuming to finalize the formalities with the investors? It went better than I imagined. This location proves to be better than the one in Los Angeles. It's at least three times the size. We plan to have a restaurant, night-club, and casino, with the largest sports betting arena in Las Vegas."

"Congratulations." She ran up and hugged him.

"Thank you. You ready to go? I want you to see the new location."

Dennis knocked on their door.

They all headed downstairs and jumped into the awaiting limousine.

With Dennis pretending to be her boyfriend, they experienced the best of what Las Vegas really had to offer. They gambled and went shopping at the finest and most exclusive designer boutiques. They headed back to the room to enjoy a quiet dinner for two.

The bellboys carefully placed her shopping bags on the sitting room couch.

She entered Brock's room with Dennis in tow, as she saw the dining room set with an elegant dinner for three, complete with burning pink candles.

Brock tipped the bellboys and they left.

"Let me change clothes and we can have dinner." Brock offered.

"You two enjoy your dinner. I'll see you tomorrow morning." Dennis kissed her on the cheek.

"Thank you Dennis, for a wonderful day." Nicole/Sabrina said.

"You're welcome. The pleasure was all ours."

"Thanks a lot, Dennis. What would I do without you?" Brock said, re-entering the room wearing a white, plush, terry cloth robe.

"How about a raise?" Dennis laughed.

"That's funny, considering you own a newer Mercedes, than I do. You want to help yourself to some food?" Brock offered Dennis.

"No, I'm going to head downstairs and gamble for a while. I might even get lucky." He winked. "You two have a great evening." He walked out of the door.

Brock sat down at the table for dinner. He served her a plate of food, and then he served himself. They begin to eat.

"So where do you see yourself, in five years from now?" Brock asked during dinner.

Nicole was lost in his eyes. "I'm sorry, did you say something?"

"I said, where do you see yourself in five years, Sabrina?"

"I have no idea. Hopefully, after five years, I will have become a complete woman, maybe, with a husband, and a couple of children, from his previous marriage."

"You really want to have the operation? You're perfect just the way that you are. There are some real women who wish they could look as good as you. You could definitely use more in the breast department. Other than that, I really wouldn't tamper with perfection."

"You're on the outside, looking in. You have no idea

of what it feels like to be me; having to hide a certain part of your anatomy, because it doesn't belong on the woman I envision for myself. I feel like I have been running my entire life, and I am so close to the finish line. I want to finish what I have started. And by the way, my name is Nicole. I told you earlier that I'm in the process of having it legally changed. Sabrina is my ad name."

"Nicole is much better. Nicole, I like you just the way you are." He smiled.

"And I really like you, too."

"I think that you are too good of a person to live the life that you are currently living."

"I would say that I agree with you, one hundred percent. I don't plan on being an escort forever. I am very serious about reaching my goal."

"Would you allow me to make it easier for you?"

"How?"

"I would like you to refrain from soliciting yourself and allow me to assist you in obtaining your goals. I am willing to provide everything for you, even furnish you with a car of your choice. I want to take care of you, until you decide what you want to do with your life."

"I can take care of myself at Peppa's house."

"You will continue to sell yourself at Peppa's house. I don't want you to do that anymore. You have the potential to become a great artist. Maybe that's what you need to focus on. You are so talented and beautiful. It would be an honor to provide for you, future, world-renowned artist."

"Can I ask you something?"

"Please, be my guest."

"So, what would you get out of the deal?"

"Of course, I would get to see you whenever I could get away to San Diego. You would still have your privacy. You would no longer have to risk your safety and well-being with numerous, strange men. You would be able to create and explore your artistic abilities, without distraction, or the temptation of prostitution. Have you even considered going back to school? Better yet, what about art school? I will provide your full tuition, and funding, with all the necessary instruments and utensils. Trust me, if there is an artist inside you, together, we will bring it out."

"Why me? You can have any girl you want."

"I stopped dating the women in LA, because they all desire to be a celebrity, or a celebrity's wife. They are all pretentious, high-maintenance, blatant, fortune seekers, and then I met you. You were a breath of fresh air; beautiful, talented, and down to earth. In addition to being incredibly sexy, you passed the test."

"What test?"

"When I offered you the tennis bracelet, you turned it down. That has never happened before, and that is when you really impressed me. Why did you turn it down?"

"I guess, I thought I really didn't deserve it. You had already paid for my time, what more could I ask for?"

"And that is why I want to help you."

"Can I think about it?"

"Sure. Take your time."

———

Nicole returned to San Diego, and informed Peppa of her good news.

"But Peppa, he really likes me."

"I understand that, but you will still be a prostitute in his eyes." Peppa argued.

"At least, I will only have to have sex with one man."

"Are you sure you can trust him?"

"Yes, of course I can trust him. He is always a perfect gentleman. He has never treated me like a prostitute."

"It sounds like you are falling in love with him."

"Don't be ridiculous," Nicole laughed. "I know he's married. I'd be a fool to fall in love with Brock."

"Hi, fool." Peppa laughed.

"Peppa, that's not funny."

"I'm serious. I've been with you from the beginning. I will never turn my back on you, no matter how naïve I think you are. I want you to do what you think is best for you." Peppa hugged Nicole.

Nicole moved out of Peppa's and moved into a small, rented, secluded, three-bedroom home in Point Loma, an affluent suburb of San Diego.

Brock not only provided two years of college at the Creative Arts Institutes of California, but he insisted that she take business management and accounting courses.

He offered her full financial support and gave her total control of decorating the entire house. He also afforded her a generous monthly allowance. Brock was genuinely impressed with her self-taught, artistic abilities.

She would see Brock regularly, at least once a month, mostly on the weekends. Every visit she would share her new creations and college experiences with him.

During the first year, Brock became infatuated with her. He demanded that she enhance her small breast into a larger C-cup, from the finest plastic surgeon in Beverly Hills. He also coerced her into increasing the volume in her hips, a forehead shaving, and numerous facial dermatology treatments.

Brock truly enjoyed the time he spent with Nicole,

and often thought of leaving his wife for her. Brock knew that it would be disastrous to his reputation and his businesses.

He taught her how to drive a car, and purchased her the car of her choice. Nicole decided on a new cute little, full-sized, 4-door sedan, with a shiny rag top that was easy on gas.

She and Peppa remained very close.

Peppa helped her decorate the house.

Now that Nicole had transportation, she was able to spend more time with Peppa. They would take trips to Las Vegas and Los Angeles, when Brock wasn't in town.

Brock became insecure with Nicole's new found independence. He drove down to San Diego, unbeknownst to Nicole. He waited for her for three days. He was furious.

She noticed the rental car in the driveway when she returned home. She rushed inside to greet him. Once inside, she noticed that all of her framed art had been destroyed, ripped right off the walls. Even her art in progress and classroom assignments, had been ripped to shreds.

"Oh my God, what happened in here?! What is going on?!" Nicole screamed at Brock.

"Where the hell have you been?" He forcefully

grabbed her by the arm. "I have been waiting three fucking days for you."

She could smell alcohol on his breath.

"I'm sorry. The girls and I took a road trip to Vegas." Her heart was racing. "I would have never gone to Vegas if I knew you were coming. I'm sorry. You weren't supposed to arrive until this weekend."

He slapped her hard across the face. He grabbed her by the hair and forced her into the bedroom. He grabbed her by the throat and slammed her against the bedroom wall.

"Don't you ever forget that you are here, because I put you here."

Tears fell from her eyes.

"What I'm doing for you, I could have done for any black whore. I created you, and don't you ever forget it. Anytime you leave here from now on, I am to be informed. Do you fucking understand me?" He squeezed her neck tighter.

She shook her head, yes as she tried to loosen his grip.

"This will never happen again. Understand?" He released her.

"Yes," she cried.

"Get undressed." Brock violently pushed her back onto to the bed.

———

"That was the night that I met Brock's alter ego, the abusive alcoholic." Nicole told Michelle.

"What an asshole. He treated you just like a slave, like he owned you. Oh, girl, I hate Brock Bass. He better not show up at KNB this weekend. What time is it?" Michelle stood up and grabbed her purse and keys. "We have been here for almost two hours. We have to finish this conversation later. Thank God, my boss is an understanding man. I will call you later tonight, when I get home, Bye, Nicole." She kissed her on the cheek as she rushed from the cafeteria.

"Bye, Michelle." Nicole stood up as painful memories she suffered with Brock, flooded her mind.

FOUR

Several hours later, the phone rang at KNB Art Gallery. Nicole was putting on her coat to leave the gallery, after a long day of work. She looked at her watch. It was 7:39 pm. *Who would be calling the gallery this late?*

"Good evening, KNB Art Gallery." Nicole answered.

"Hey, Girl, it's me Michelle. I'm glad I caught you before you left. I had so much to do. I got off work and picked up the boys from afterschool childcare. Then we came home, I cooked dinner, helped the boys with their homework, and fed them. I finally have a free moment to myself, before Malik gets home from work. I have been thinking about you and Brock Bass all day. I had to find out what happened next. Did you see Brock again, after you found out he was a crazy, abusive, alcoholic?"

"Yes, I ended up going back to him." Nicole answered.

"What? What the hell could he have said, or done, to make you go back to him?"

"He paid for my reconstructive surgery. He found one of the top surgeons in Sex Reassignment Surgeries (SRS) in San Francisco, California. He paid for my all my travel expenses, and hospital recovery accommodations."

"I'm so glad you brought it up, because I have been dying to ask you about your surgery. Did the operation hurt? How long did it take? Was it a hard decision to make to cut off your penis? How do you pee?"

"Hold on, Michelle, one question at a time. To be honest Michelle, any surgery is painful once the anesthetics wear off. And trust me; the surgery was worth the pain. The entire surgery took less than four hours. It also required an additional three months to heal completely. I urinate just like any other woman, I sit down."

"How did you choose to cut off your penis?"

"I hated having a penis. Imagine yourself looking and feeling like a woman, with a penis dangling between your legs. I hated having sex with it, I felt like a freak. All the men that were attracted to my male genitals, were very unattractive to me."

"Do you feel the same sexual satisfaction with a

vagina? Can you achieve orgasm? Can you achieve multiple orgasms like a woman?"

"In the beginning, I really didn't know what to expect. Having a vagina was brand new to me. The more I explored it, the more I figured out what it could do. My doctor did an amazing job. I had my operation on February 11, 2010. I will never forget it; because that is the day I was born again. Once I healed completely, I cried the first time I saw my corrected, functional genitals. Oh my God, I never knew that sex would be so good as a woman. I have never achieved multiple orgasms, but I can climax. Brock became even more possessive, once I had the surgery. And when he was drinking, he was impossible to deal with. I knew I had to get away from him. I dropped out of school, and decided to relocate to Atlanta. I heard that Atlanta was the new Black Hollywood. I was a real woman now, without limits or boundaries. I had nearly forty thousand dollars that I saved for my operation. What a great place for an African-American, female artist to spread her wings."

"What an accomplishment, I have a whole new respect and admiration for you."

"Thank you, Michelle. It wasn't easy, but it was worth it."

"So, what are you doing now?" Michelle asked.

"I'm tired. It's been a long day. I was about to walk

out of the door, when you called. I still have to get home, and clean the house before Rashidi and his mother arrive."

"Well, I'll let you go. Thank you for sharing. Keep your head up. See you at the gallery grand opening."

"Ok, see you Friday night." She hung up. Nicole grabbed her purse and keys, set the alarm, locked the door and left the gallery.

FIVE

Nicole carefully pulled into their driveway in the Wesley Estates. She waited for the garage door to open, and pulled into the left of the garage, next to their black Escalade. She activated the electronic garage door to close as she entered the house from the garage.

She remembered the day they signed the paperwork for the house. Because of the sizeable amount of their down payment, they purchased the home of their dreams.

Isaiah encouraged Nicole to decorate the house as she saw fit if she included him a relaxed, comfortable game room.

She slowly ascended the staircase to their double-door bedroom. Nicole placed her keys and purse on the soft gray lacquer dresser and headed for the bath room. She turned on the light in the spacious bathroom. She turned on the water in the Jacuzzi styled, sunken bath-tub, adding a generous amount of fragrant, relaxation beads.

She walked into the large closet on the right side of the bathroom. She braced herself against the closet wall and removed her boots, placing her boots in their proper acrylic box. After removing all of her clothing, she threw it all into the hamper. She would take the dirty clothes down to the laundry room, after her shower.

She walked back into the main part of the bathroom.

"How are you?" Isaiah asked, standing in the bath-room doorway.

Nicole jumped. She didn't hear him come in. She quickly grabbed a towel off the towel rack.

"I'm ok. I didn't hear you come in." She answered as she wrapped up, walking past him. "Excuse me."

"Go ahead." He continued to stare directly at her.

She dropped the towel, and entered the hot, soothing bath water. She laid back into the water.

Isaiah sat next to her on the edge of the tub, concealing his arousal. "Did Rashidi call you today?" He desperately wanted to make love to her. He felt his penis throbbing, straining against his fitted boxers.

"Yes." This is the closest she had been to Isaiah in weeks. Her body yearned for his masculine touch.

He looked so sexy in his grungy, work clothes.

She could smell his strong masculine scent over the fragrant bath water. Her erect nipples were hidden under the bubbles.

"Are you cool with Yvonne coming to Atlanta?" He asked her.

The way he uses his lips is so sexy.

"If it doesn't bother you, it doesn't bother me. I love when Rashidi is here. His energetic personality brightens up the whole house."

"While Yvonne is here, I will try to convince her to let him stay."

"That's a great idea."

"So, what's up with us?" He asked as he caressed her soft shoulder.

She leaned forward and turned off the water.

"What do you mean, what's up with us?"

Their eyes locked.

He leaned forward and kissed her softly on the mouth. He licked her lips, and pulled back slowly.

"I've had a lot of time to think about us. I appreciate you giving me time to think. The past couple of weeks have been tough for me, and I'm sure they have been hell for you, too. You are my best friend, and my business partner. Nicole, you have always been a woman to me, but not just any woman, you're my woman. I love you. I can't help it."

"I love you, too, Isaiah." She threw her wet arms around his neck as she kissed him passionately.

He held her tightly as he kissed her back.

They hungrily fed on each other, relenting to their pent-up passion. They made love in the tub, and once again in the bed.

Isaiah awoke with Nicole's head resting on his chest. He kissed her lightly on the forehead, waking her up.

"What time is it?" She asked.

"I don't know, but I have to take a leak." Isaiah rose quickly from the bed and rushed into the bathroom. "It's 3:10 in the morning." He spoke loudly from the bathroom. "You hungry? I'm starving. You want me to run to the Waffle House? It's too late to cook."

"I don't mind. There are some thawed out pork chops in the refrigerator. I can whip up some rice and gravy real fast to go with them. Sound good?"

"Hell, yeah."

She got out of bed and walked past him into the shower. After her quick shower, she dried off in the closet. She put on long flowing pink robe as he blocked her inside the closet. She walked up and faced him.

"What?" She smiled up at him.

"Do you know that I loved you the first moment I laid eyes on you?"

"Yes, I felt the same way," she hugged him around his naked waist.

"Now, can I get into the kitchen, so I can feed this hungry man that loves me so much?"

"I'll go with you."

She headed downstairs to the kitchen. She was elated; she couldn't wait to tell Michelle that she was right.

Isaiah took a quick shower and put on a pair of plaid, loose-fitting, pajama bottoms. He joined Nicole in the kitchen, sitting on one of the barstools.

"Want something to drink?" She asked.

"Water." He answered.

She reached into the fridge and handed him a bottle of water. She had already started frying the pork chops.

He could smell them. He drank the water.

She handed him another one. "Can I help you with something?" Isaiah asked.

"I got it. You're fine where you are." She stirred the gravy and onions.

"So are you." He replied.

She turned around and smiled at him. "I've been thinking, I insist that Yvonne should stay in a hotel. Maybe not the first night, Rashidi would want his mother with us. For the remainder of the weekend, she will stay in a hotel."

"What made you say that? I didn't bring her name up, but now that you've mentioned her, I'm looking forward to meeting the woman who bore your only child. What should I expect?" Nicole questioned.

"I don't know. I haven't seen her in years. And when I did see her, it was to pick up my son."

"What was she like? You obviously loved her at one point in your life."

"She was aw'ight in the looks department."

"I'm sure you can do better than that."

"Ok, she was fine. Keep in mind that was 13 years ago, when we were together. She was tall, with long legs like yours."

"That's a little better. What about the rest of her? Did she have a nice body? Was she pretty? Not just her appearance, was she a good person?"

"She was aw'ight; creamy, medium-brown complexion."

"Creamy, hunh?"

"Hey, you asked. Can I finish, please?"

"I'm sorry for interrupting. Please continue."

"She was about 5'8, not really thick, but at the same time, she wasn't skinny either. She was perfect."

Nicole stifled a remark.

"She should have been a model. Her father was a big-time drug dealer. She always had the best of everything. Yvonne acted like some kind of Nubian princess. She had this attitude, a way about herself, kind of classy, and snobbish, and at the same time, sensitive and vulnerable. I guess that's what made her so appealing. Every dude in school was trying to get with her, and she wanted me. She was the first girl I ever had sex with. My mother hated her from day one, but I loved her. When she told me she was pregnant with my child, I asked her to marry me. A month later, I caught my first case. Yvonne's father hired me the best lawyer money could buy and got the case dismissed. That's when I started working for her father; not only to thank him for what he had done for me, but to prove to him, I was worthy of his daughter. Later that year, we both graduated from high school. We moved into our own place. Yvonne hadn't given birth yet, and she became more and more demanding. I had to take greater risks, in order to earn greater dividends. I was becoming quite influential in the drug game. I wasn't no fool though. I put away more money than I spent. If Yvonne had known that, she would have spent that, too. Anyway, to make a long story short, I got busted again. At the same time, her family got hit. If Yvonne had been living with her family, she and my unborn son would have been killed, too."

"What? Her whole family?"

"Everybody, her mother, father, younger sister and brother."

"Damn, that's horrible."

"And there was nothing I could do about it. I was originally sentenced to five years in prison. I received additional time for killing an inmate for attempted rape. In the beginning, Yvonne was there for me. Then one day, she stopped accepting my calls, no more letters, no more visits. She finally wrote me a letter and told me she met someone. Yvonne got married and that really fucked me up. The only reason I made it through prison was because of my son. Ten years later, after I was released from prison, I was introduced to my ten-year-old son, Rashidi. She did a hell of a job raising my son. That alone removed the deep hatred I felt for her. I owe her the upmost respect for the healthy, intelligent and perfect son, she rose in my absence."

"So she has some good qualities?" Nicole asked.

"I guess so."

"Did she ever have any more children?"

"I don't know."

"Do you know why Yvonne wants to visit Atlanta, all of a sudden?"

"I'm hoping that she is realizing that Rashidi is growing up, and he needs his father, to become a man."

"And an awesome father you are." Nicole smiled at Isaiah.

"Thank you, that means a lot to me. Everything I do is for Rashidi."

She walked over and kissed him.

"So, how's the gallery coming along?" He asked.

"Better than I expected. Without you, I had no other choice but to throw myself into my work. I finished one series and started a new one. I call it, 'The Future.' Different children are dressed in adult career attire. I took pictures of Rashidi dressed in his Easter suit, looking just like you. I call it 'Future President'. I'll show it to you." She held up a framed print of the drawing that was on the kitchen table. She brought it home to hang in the house. Isaiah's mouth fell open, looking at the drawing.

"My baby is so damn talented." He walked in the kitchen and kissed Nicole on the cheek. "This is mine, I love it. Rashidi is going to have a fit when he sees this." Isaiah exclaimed. "I'll hang it up, tomorrow."

"You're welcome. I also drew one of Malik Jr, dressed in his Halloween football costume. I call that one, 'Future MVP'."

"My lady is so talented. I can't wait to see it."

"I nearly had to fight Michelle to keep the one of

Malik Jr. I promised her that she could have it, after I showcase it in the gallery."

"Do you have everything you need?"

"The entire gallery is pretty much set. I've been adding finishing touches, here and there."

"Is that an invitation for me to come into the gallery later on today?"

"I would really like that. I wouldn't have a gallery grand opening if it weren't for you. I have always honored your opinion."

He kissed her again.

"How are the books at Complete Care?" She asked him.

"I was hoping you would ask me that. When can you come in the shops and check over the books?"

"I can stop by before I go into the gallery. How is business?"

"It's been busy since we returned from Cali. Your idea about advertising and marketing to women, in women magazines as the trustworthy mechanic, has increased business by 40 percent. You know Mr. Wilson--Chuck from Chuck's garage asked about you. I told him about the gallery opening this weekend."

"I sent him and his wife an invitation. What did he say?"

"He asked when we were going to get married."

"What did you say?"

"I told him that we decided to postpone it, that we wanted to open the gallery first. He also said that someone else might snatch you up. And that really made me think. Could I imagine my life without you in it? Which brings me to the Brock Bass situation; if he comes around, I promise you that I am going to seriously hurt him."

"I think you're all overreacting. BB is here in Atlanta to open a new sports bar, and that's all there is to it. How does Brock know that I live in Atlanta? How would he know about you and your business?"

"It's more than a coincidence. Less than a month ago, we received the first manila envelope. Then a second one sent to my mother's house. Thank God she didn't open it, and sent it to us. The information in that envelope would have blown her deeply religious mind."

"It seems someone is out to get you, not me." Nicole replied.

"You might be right. Who is the question?" Isaiah asked.

Six

"Mom, look how high we are. Those cars look like toys." Rashidi exclaimed, as he looked out of the airplane window.

Yvonne, who was seated next to him, was elated and relieved that they were preparing to land in Atlanta. It seemed they had been on this flight from Florida forever.

"Rashidi, now you know how I hate to fly. Why does it take so long to descend?"

"Relax Mom, we're almost there. You're really going to like Nicole. She is so cool."

"What makes her so cool? Is it because she is going to marry your father?"

"No, she's cool because she doesn't act like adults do all the time. She's more like a friend. We all play videogames and watch movies, until the sun comes up."

"We do that." Yvonne responded.

"But you're my mother; you're supposed to do that."

"Oh really?" Yvonne laughed.

"She's just fun to be with. She makes me laugh."

"I don't make you laugh?"

"Yeah, but I make her laugh, too."

"You make me laugh all the time." Yvonne prodded her son.

"I know, but Nicole makes Dad happy, too."

"Really?" She asked her son.

"We are going to have so much fun. I promise, you are really going to like Nicole."

"If you feel that strongly about her, I'm sure that I will like her."

"You will, I promise." Rashidi resumed looking out of the airplane window, anticipating the impact of landing back on the ground.

Yvonne was looking forward to seeing Isaiah again. She regretted how their relationship ended, and what she did to him. She truly loved Isaiah, but how can you truly love a man without physical intimacy? A woman has needs, and his incarceration did not eliminate her needs. She didn't plan to fall in love with Derrick. Derrick was intended as a temporary replacement for Isaiah. They were married two months later; she had her son to think about. Derrick was not only an Officer in the military, but a good man, and a great father figure. Even though she was married to Derrick, the only man she would ever truly love was Isaiah. She wished she loved Derrick the way she loved Isaiah.

Once Isaiah was released from prison, Yvonne tried to end their marriage. Derrick made it difficult for her to leave, and reluctantly agreed to their separation, three years later. Yvonne packed up her and Rashidi's belongings and moved out into an economy lodge. *Now that I am separated from Derrick; I will get Isaiah back, no matter who gets in my way.*

———

Nicole and Isaiah pulled into the entrance of the parking facility at Hartsfield International Airport.

"I can't wait to see Rashidi. I wonder has he gotten any taller?" Nicole asked Isaiah.

"It's only been three months. I'm sure he will let us know."

"He wants to be as tall as his father."

"He will be, it's in the Mathis blood."

"The weather should be perfect this weekend. Have you planned anything special for Yvonne and Rashidi?" She asked.

"How about dinner tonight at the Cheesecake Factory?"

"Don't they require a reservation?"

"What about the Atlanta Fish Market?"

"They're both good. Let me call them on my cell." She dialed directory assistance and made the calls. "They accept reservations, but they are not required."

"Good. So, which one?" He asked.

"Cheesecake, I like the atmosphere there. You should take Rashidi to Fun Zone out in Roswell."

"What's Fun Zone?"

"It's a huge arcade, movie theater and mini-amusement park. Rashidi will love it."

"Sounds like fun. How did you hear about it?"

"I went with Michelle, Malik and the kids."

"Aren't you going to go with us?"

"I think it would make it special, if you and Rashidi went alone, male bonding. I could take Yvonne shopping at one of the malls."

"It won't be any fun without you."

"We could go after I close the gallery. I don't want to make everyone wait for me."

"You know I'm going to wait for you." He said.

"Speaking of the gallery, what happened to you? I waited for you." She said as Isaiah parked the SUV.

"I planned on coming in, but I was so busy with your surprise."

"Surprise?" Nicole asked.

"Surprises, I should have said. I've been working on it for a while now. Don't even think about asking me what it is. I figured that I will see the gallery for the first time, just like everybody else. This is your gift to the world and your dream. I want to be right by your side, when the world is introduced to the remarkable talents of Mrs. Nicole Mathis."

Nicole smiled. "What did you say?"

"I said your remarkable talents." Isaiah responded innocently.

"After that, what did you call me?" She asked.

"I said your name."

"Say it again."

"Say what again?"

"My name, Isaiah."

"Nicole." He teased.

"My whole name."

"Nicole Bennett. Happy now?"

"You said, Mrs. Nicole Mathis."

"Did I?"

She playfully punched him in the chest.

Isaiah started laughing.

"Yes, you did."

They unbuckled their seatbelts and exited the truck.

Nicole was wearing a soft brown, long-sleeved cable-knit, sweater-dress. Her dress was belted at the waist with dark brown leggings, and dark-brown, high-heeled boots. Her long, naturally curly hair was flowing in the cool night air.

Isaiah wore a black silk, dress shirt, black wide-leg slacks, black dress shoes and a large black leather coat. He walked around to her side of the black SUV and opened the door for her.

"I don't give a fuck about your past. I need you in my life forever. I love you for who you are today. Nicole, will you please marry me?" Isaiah got down on one knee and slid the four carat diamond ring back onto her finger.

Nicole didn't know that Isaiah kept the ring.

"Yes!" she screamed. He stood up and kissed her openly in the mouth. "I love you so much, Isaiah." He wrapped his massive arm around her waist as they walked towards the arrival terminal.

———

"Come on, Mom."

"Rashidi, will you please slow down, there's no need

to run." Yvonne said, as Rashidi ran back to her, and grabbed her by the hand.

He started tugging her forward.

"Rashidi, please. You're going to ruin my outfit." Yvonne wore a tight, revealing sweater, trimmed in mink, tight black jeans and high-heeled black designer boots. She carried a mid-size, black and gold matching, designer handbag. She wore her black and gold sunglasses in her hair as the sunglasses held back her relaxed, shoulder-length tresses.

Rashidi wore a red, black, and white warm-up suit with matching tennis shoes. He had a red, black, and white, backpack hung over his shoulder.

"Look Mom, there they are!" Rashidi exclaimed.

Yvonne looked up ahead and saw Isaiah. She couldn't refrain from smiling.

Rashidi let go of her hand and ran towards his father. "Dad!"

Yvonne was astonished at how age improved Isaiah's appearance. She noticed that he was clean-cut and groomed to perfection. He exuded a masculine confidence. He was even sexier today, she thought to herself.

"Hey, Dad." Rashidi embraced his father.

"What up, man?" He hugged his son tightly. Isaiah noticed the small twists in his son's hair. The beginning stages of dreadlocks. Rashidi released his father and hugged Nicole.

"Hi, Nicole."

"Hi, Rashidi. It's so nice to see you again. You look so handsome. I love the twists." Isaiah looked at Nicole, disapprovingly.

"Thank you." Rashidi smiled at her.

"They make you look so mature." Nicole added.

"That's what Mom says." Rashidi responded.

Yvonne finally reached the group. "Hello, Isaiah."

Isaiah extended his hand to Yvonne.

Yvonne hugged Isaiah, tightly.

Isaiah looked at Nicole, like what the hell.

"How you doing, Yvonne? How was your flight?" Isaiah said, suddenly placed in an awkward position.

Yvonne took a step back and gazed at him.

"Damn, you look good. It's so nice to be on the ground again." She turned and faced Nicole. "And you must be the artist responsible for creating this master-piece. Nicole, right? It's so nice to finally meet you." She decided to hug Nicole as well, to masquerade her intentions. "Rashidi talks about you all the time."

"Hello. Welcome to Atlanta." Nicole said as Yvonne released her.

"I hate to fly. I thought we would never land. Rashidi was pointing and talking the whole flight. Mom, look at that, look how high we are, did you feel that? I could have strangled him."

Nicole and Isaiah laughed.

Nicole never imagined that Yvonne would be so poised and beautiful. She noticed her perfectly manicured hands, which reminded Nicole to get her nails done.

Yvonne has a fashion model's composure; a classy, pampered elegance about herself. Her flawless cocoa-brown complexion glowed as if she were in a cosmetic magazine advertisement. Her figure was stunning; large, full bust line, small waist with shapely hips and rear end.

Nicole became conscientious of her own weight.

"I love your outfit. Are you wearing Gucci?" Nicole asked.

"Yes, thank you. I picked up this ensemble on vacation in Las Vegas." She smiled at Nicole. This bitch is breathtaking, Yvonne thought to herself. "Rashidi says that you're the best artist in the world."

Nicole smiled at Rashidi. "An artist is only as good as her subjects." Nicole responded.

"I look forward to seeing more of your work." Yvonne added.

"Rashidi and I are going to get the luggage. You two get better acquainted." Isaiah said as he kissed Nicole on the lips. "We'll meet you at the truck." He handed the truck keys to Nicole.

"Ok." Nicole smiled at him.

Rashidi kissed his mother on the cheek. "We'll be back."

"Bye, son."

"Bye, Rashidi." Nicole said as she and Yvonne casually strolled towards thru the terminal, towards the parking lot.

"So where do you live in Florida?" Nicole asked Yvonne.

"We live in Fort Walton Beach, about six hours from Orlando. My husband was an Officer in the military, Officer Derrick Reynolds. Now he's a Sergeant in the Fort Walton Beach Police Department."

"Why didn't you bring him? We have more than enough room."

"We've been separated for three months," Yvonne lied. Rashidi didn't tell you?" Yvonne acted surprise.

"No, Rashidi didn't mention it. Are you ok?"

"I'm fine. Our marriage had run its course. I'm surprised Derrick stayed with me that long. He really wanted more children. He will be an excellent father. He has helped me in so many ways with Rashidi. I'm just not ready or willing to have another child. It took me years to lose that baby fat. Why don't you and Isaiah have children?"

"Isaiah feels the same way you do. Rashidi is enough for him."

Yvonne smiled at Nicole. "What about you? Don't you want children?"

"I do. Unfortunately, I can't have children."

"I'm sorry. That must hard to deal with?"

"I have to accept it, what else can I do? We could always adopt. It makes it easier to love and appreciate other people's children."

"That makes sense. No wonder Rashidi is so fond of you."

"I love Rashidi. He's a great kid. You have done an excellent job raising him."

""Well, thank you. Rashidi is a good kid, he makes parenting so easy. He brings such joy into my life. I feel that's why we are so close."

"He absolutely adores you." Nicole admired.

"The only bad thing is, he's turning into a mommas' boy. He is just like his father. I had to pry Isaiah away from his mother and trust me it wasn't easy. His mother hated me. So, I'm preparing for the day when some woman will pry Rashidi away from me."

"So what do you do in Fort Walton Beach?"

"I'm the customer service manager, with the local

phone company. I've been with them ever since Rashidi started preschool."

"Are you hungry? Isaiah wants to take us to dinner."

"Sounds good, where?"

"The Cheesecake Factory."

"I've heard of it, but I have never eaten there before."

"You'll love it. It is really nice, in a casual setting. They serve excellent food and desserts."

"Good, I'm starving. I haven't eaten since we left home."

A handsome, well dressed, middle-aged African American male approached them. "Good evening, ladies. How are you two doing this evening?"

"Hello," they said in unison. Yvonne surveyed him and concluded that he was attractive.

"Are you both visiting Atlanta?" He asked.

"I am," Yvonne replied.

"I live here." Nicole replied.

"My name is Winston Horne. And your names are?"

"Yvonne."

"Nicole."

"Beautiful names, for beautiful ladies."

"Thank you." They spoke.

"I'm here in Atlanta for business. Can I convince the both of you into having dinner with me this evening?" Winston asked.

"I'm sorry; I'm here with my fiancée." Nicole quickly answered, admiring the ring that Isaiah had just replaced on her finger.

"I'm also unavailable; it was nice meeting you though." Yvonne said.

Her response puzzled Nicole. She knew that Yvonne was recently separated. What a better way to enjoy a new environment, with a new acquaintance. Maybe, it was too soon for her to start dating, Nicole thought.

"Well, here's my card in case you change your mind." He handed his business card to Yvonne. "I will be in town until Wednesday." He smiled seductively at Yvonne.

Nicole decided to play matchmaker for Yvonne. She reached inside of her purse and handed Mr. Horne a postcard flyer. The flyer advertised her art and announced her gallery grand opening. "Maybe you would like to attend my gallery grand opening, tomorrow night."

"This is your work, Nicole?" Winston said, admiring her artwork on the flyer. "You are extremely talented. Very nice."

"Thank you."

"Are you going to attend the grand opening, Yvonne?"

"Yes, of course, that's why I'm here."

"Then I will see you there. Thank you for the invite. Have a great evening, ladies."

"Thank you. You do the same." Yvonne said.

Nicole waved goodbye.

Winston walked away.

"He was handsome. So are all the men here in Atlanta, that aggressive?"

"Not just the men, the women, too. They will approach your man with you standing there with him. I met Isaiah three weeks after I moved here. I never really had the chance to date anyone else."

"Rashidi told me that you were from California, San Diego, right?"

"Yes."

"So what brought you to Atlanta? Why would you want to leave sunny California, for Georgia?"

"I guess I wanted a fresh start. Why not Atlanta? I heard it was a fast developing city for progressive African-Americans; a place for a fledgling artist to spread her wings."

Yvonne didn't believe her. She would make it her business to find out the real reason. "How long have you been an artist?" Yvonne asked.

"Ever since I can remember, I have loved to draw. I started drawing as a hobby, something I enjoyed doing for myself. A friend of mine encouraged me to go to art school, but it was Isaiah that truly inspired me to take the art to the next level. Behind my back, Isaiah entered me in my very first art show. He started getting me orders for custom artwork. He really believes in my artistic abilities. I guess we'll see tomorrow."

"How did you meet Isaiah?"

"We met at a gas station."

"Are you serious?'

"Yes. And we have been together ever since."

They walked out of the automatic double door exit into the cool night air.

"It's cold out here." Yvonne commented.

"Trust me. It gets a lot worse. Thank God you won't be here in the winter months."

That's what you think, Yvonne thought to herself.

"The truck is right over there." Nicole pointed out.

"So, what's up with the twists?" Isaiah asked his son, referring to his hair.

"I told Mom you wouldn't like them." Rashidi answered.

"It's not that I don't like them. I'm just not used to them, yet. Does your mother like them?"

"She thinks they make me look more mature."

"I guess they do. Do you like them, is the question?"

"I do." Rashidi smiled at his father.

"Then that's all that matters. I will never tell how

you should wear your hair. That's all a part of becoming a man. You have to make your own decisions concerning your life. When I was about your age, I had a Jheri curl. I wore that curl for years."

"A Jheri Curl?" Rashidi laughed.

"My curl was bangin', I don't know who you think you're laughing at. I'm sure Grandma still has some of those pictures of me with my curl. Ask your mother about my curl."

"I can't picture my dad with a Jheri curl." Rashidi laughed.

"I did, and damn proud of it. One day, when you become a man, you will look back over your youth, and your son will laugh at you, too."

"I'm not laughing at you, I'm just laughing."

"Whatever." He playfully pushed Rashidi in the back of the head.

"Dad, can I ask you something?"

"What's up?"

"There's this girl at school that I really like."

Isaiah smiled. "I knew this day was coming. What's her name?"

"Cynthia."

"Cynthia, what? She doesn't have a last name?"

"Cynthia Ramirez, she's Spanish."

"What's up with Spanish? They don't have any black girls at your school?"

"Of course there are black girls, I just like Cynthia the most." Rashidi smiled.

"Why?"

"You sound like Mom. I don't know why, I just do."

"Is it because she's a different race than you are, her complexion, the texture of her hair, what?"

"I guess, I like her because she's fun to be with, and the way that she looks."

"Have you kissed her yet?"

"She kisses on me."

"Son, let me tell you a little something about life and women. Life is already going to be difficult for you. A young black male has many obstacles to overcome growing up as a black man. I believe television, movies, the media, even video games, are brainwashing our black youths into believing that we are no longer desirable to one another. It is important for you to remember that someone of your own race has the same background that you have. That doesn't make them necessarily better for you; it just means that you will have a mutual foundation to build on."

"So you're saying that I should stick with my own kind?"

"I would prefer that your first experience with girls

would be of your own race. I say that because you should experience a relationship with your own race, rather than developing a negative attitude towards our black women without even knowing why. But this is your life. I want you to live the life that you choose. I have seen beautiful women in all races. I knew at a young age, that I wanted my wife or girlfriend, to be of my own race. That may not be what you want."

"Mom makes it seem so bad."

"It probably is, to her. Your mother is a beautiful, proud black woman and I'm sure she wants you to marry a girl that resembles her. This might go over your head, but I'm going to say it to you anyway. Imagine, you are a grown man, and you and your African American wife, have a daughter. Imagine, your daughter brings home Caucasian, Hispanic or Asian guys; every nationality except your own race, and you're her father. How would that make you feel, as her father?"

Rashidi thought about the question. "Maybe, she was ashamed of her race. Or black men weren't attractive, or good enough for her. Or she might be ashamed of me."

"Very good. It bothers me when I see successful, African American men and women, married or dating outside of their race. It makes me think that they are ashamed of their race or that their own race isn't good enough. I understand that love is not a color, and you can't help who you fall in love with. But there are young black men your age that would never consider dating a girl of their own race, and that really bothers me. What kind of shit is that? Another lesson you will learn in life, is that happiness comes from making the right choices, at the right time. It's not about pleasing your mother and me. It's about pleasing Rashidi, and hopefully the choices you make, will make us both proud." Isaiah hugged his son.

"I love you, Dad." Rashidi hugged him back.

"I love you too, son."

SEVEN

After dinner, they all arrived at the home of Nicole and Isaiah.

Dinner went well and put Isaiah at ease. He opened the garage door with the remote attached to the sun visor in the truck. He parked the SUV in the garage to the right of Nicole's car. Isaiah exited the truck and quickly ran to the passenger's side, to open the door for Nicole.

Rashidi jumped out.

"I'll get the luggage, Dad." Rashidi offered.

"Ok, son. Put your mother's luggage in the upstairs guestroom."

"Thank you," Nicole said.

Isaiah kissed her as he assisted her out. He also opened the door for Yvonne.

"Thank you," Yvonne smiled seductively as she took a hold of his hand.

"No problem," Isaiah smiled. He helped Rashidi with the luggage and walked inside the house.

"This is nice," Yvonne said, referring to Nicole's car. "I love your car, girl. I drive a Lexus, too. How did you get it that shade of pink?"

"This was my one year anniversary gift from Isaiah; he did the customized paint job."

"That's Isaiah for you. He's always had a fascination with cars. Just like his father. I think Rashidi will follow in his father's footsteps."

"Like father, like son." Nicole agreed. "Let me show you the house."

She and Yvonne walked into their home from the garage entrance.

Nicole spent all morning cleaning; making sure the entire house was spotless.

"This is beautiful. It's so warm and inviting." Yvonne admired.

"This is the den. Isaiah insisted that it should be very comfortable." Nicole explained.

The large spacious room was decorated in several shades of brown. The walls were all painted a light pale brown, which accented the immense, dark brown, sectional sofa. To the right of the room was a fireplace.

Several ornate, wooden pieces of African-art adorned the fireplace mantel. In front of the sectional sofa, there was an ultra-modern, wood and glass, coffee table, littered with remote controls.

In front of the table sat a gigantic, wood and glass, wall unit, equipped with a 55' flat screen television. The wall unit shelves held a Blue ray combination player and recorder, high-definition, cable box and every video game system presently offered on the market. To the left and right of the wall-unit, tall, open-faced, wooden, storage shelving racks were filled to capacity with the latest video games and movies.

Immediately, Yvonne noticed the drawing of Rashidi, in a basic black frame, above the fireplace mantel.

"Oh my God, when did you do this?" She walked up to the drawing.

"I drew it last month. Didn't it turn out wonderful? This is my new favorite piece."

"Nicole, I love this. When did he take this picture? I have to have this." Yvonne turned to face Nicole.

"This is a print. I have the original displayed in the gallery. I took this picture the last time he was here. I asked Rashidi to pretend that he was the President of the United States of America. The pose and facial expression was all Rashidi's idea. It's a part of my future series."

"This isn't the original?" She turned around to look at the piece again. "The details are incredible. Your drawing is incredible." She faced Nicole again. "I will not take no for an answer."

"It's my favorite, Yvonne." Nicole pleaded.

Yvonne grabbed a hold of Nicole's hands.

"Please, sell it to me. You name the price. Whatever you want, I have to have it. Please." She begged.

"If it means that much to you, I guess I can part with it," Nicole smiled. "You can have it."

Yvonne embraced Nicole. "Thank you, thank you, thank you." Rashidi and Isaiah walked into the den. "Rashidi, come here. Did you see this? Did you know that Nicole drew this picture of you?"

Rashidi gawked at his own drawn image. "Whoa! Nicole, you got mad skills! I think this is the best drawing you have ever done." He hugged Nicole. "I look good." They all laughed.

"Rashidi, you didn't tell me that Nicole drew like this. She is amazing."

"Yes, I did. I told she was a great artist." Rashidi said. Isaiah walked up and wrapped his arm around Nicole.

"I never imagined that she was this talented." Yvonne looked at Isaiah.

"If you're impressed with this, wait until you see

what she has in the gallery tomorrow." Isaiah said with pride.

"Girl, how do you do this?" Yvonne asked Nicole.

"I believe my talent is a gift from God."

"You know I just purchased this piece from Nicole?" Yvonne informed Isaiah.

Isaiah looked at Nicole.

"I thought it was your favorite?" Isaiah asked Nicole.

"It is, but I'm sure Yvonne will cherish it, and give it a good home."

"I will, I will. I promise. How much is it going to cost me?"

"I'm giving it to you. Consider it, a welcome to Atlanta, present."

"Thank you." Yvonne hugged Nicole away from Isaiah.

"You're welcome. Can I show you the rest of the house?" Nicole offered.

"Please." Yvonne hooked her arm through Nicole's.

They walked in from the den, to the spacious kitchen, and dining area.

"This is really nice; did you decorate yourself?" Yvonne asked.

"I did most of the house. Isaiah helped me with the den, the office upstairs, and the living room."

"I love this kitchen. You keep everything so clean."

"Let me show you the living room." Nicole showed Yvonne the rest of the house.

Nicole walked into the den, forty-five minutes later.

Isaiah and Rashidi are playing basketball on one of the video game systems, sitting on the couch.

"Who's winning?" She asked them.

"I'm letting Rashidi rack up a few points, before I punish him with my new moves." Isaiah responded.

"Yeah, right." Rashidi added. "Where's Mom?" He asked Nicole, without looking away from the television.

"She is upstairs taking a shower. Can I get my two, favorite guys something to drink?"

"I'll take a beer." Isaiah said.

"I'll have one, too," Rashidi added.

Isaiah put the game on pause, and they both looked at Rashidi.

"You'll take this ass-kickin', I'm about to put on you." His father said as he resumed the game.

"Can I have a coke, please?" Rashidi laughed.

"Of course you can. Would you like it in a glass?"

"The can."

"Me, too." Isaiah added.

Nicole always enjoyed being in the same room with the Mathis men. She loved to witness the mutual love they shared for one another. It was as though they were never apart. She retrieved their canned sodas from the refrigerator. After wiping off the mouths of the sodas, she walked back into the den.

Isaiah had moved the coffee table to the other side of the room, so both of them would have plenty of room to stretch out in front of the television.

"Here you go guys." She said as she placed their drinks on coasters on the coffee table.

Nicole turned to walk away.

"Where are you going?" Isaiah asked, focused on the television screen.

"I am going upstairs, to check on Yvonne. Make sure she doesn't need anything."

"Come here, sit down." Isaiah spread his long, muscular legs apart, and Nicole sat on the carpeted floor in front of him. He puts his arms around her, with the controller in her face as he continued to play basketball. He kissed her on her neck.

"Dad, you're cheating! You fouled me!" Rashidi yelled.

Isaiah laughed.

Rashidi playfully punched his father on his shoulder.

"Nicole, made me do it."

"Don't blame me, Isaiah." Nicole playfully elbowed Isaiah on his leg.

"Ya'll better quit hitting on me." Isaiah said as he dropped the controller and lunged for Rashidi.

Rashidi dropped his controller, and attacked his father.

Nicole stood up and jumped on Isaiah's back.

They were having fun laughing and wrestling with each other.

Yvonne suddenly appeared in the kitchen entryway, dripping wet, wrapped only in light green, terry-cloth towel, barely covering up her body. All three of them froze as they stared at her.

"I need to borrow your blow dryer." Yvonne calmly replied.

EIGHT

Nicole laid in her bed thinking about the gallery grand opening. She was nervous and excited. She peered over at the digital alarm clock that sat on the nightstand next to her bed. It read 8:37 am. Isaiah had already left for work.

The ringing of the house phone broke the quiet.

"Hello?" Nicole answered.

"Good morning, baby. You excited? Today is your big day." Gladys Mathis said to her.

"Good morning, Mama Mathis. I wish that you were here. It won't be the same without you."

"You know my health ain't what it used to be. I promise to God that I developed a heart condition when my husband died. But don't you worry, I prayed about the gallery opening. I will be there in spirit."

"You know that your grandson is here." Nicole informed her.

"My grandbaby, Rashidi, is there? I should have forced myself to get there. Now, I'm mad at myself. Please, let me talk to him."

"I'm sorry, I'm sure he left this morning to go to work with his father. You know the Mathis men are inseparable. You can call him at work."

"Ok, I will."

"You need the number?"

"I have it. God is going to bless you, so you will be very prosperous tonight, baby."

"Thank you, Mama Mathis. You hurry up and get well, so you can come to Atlanta and see the gallery. I have taken plenty of pictures. I will send them to you."

"Oh, thank you, baby. Ya'll are so good to me."

"You're welcome and don't forget to call Rashidi."

"I'm calling as soon as I hang up with you. Love you, Nicole."

"I love you, too, Mama Mathis."

Nicole decided to get up and start her day. Her schedule today was tight. She had two appointments for her hair and nails.

She heard a soft knock on her bedroom door. "Come in."

"Good morning, girl." Yvonne walked in. "I'm

sorry again about last night, dripping water everywhere." She lied, pleased with her performance. She saw the way Isaiah looked at her, she just knew he wanted her back.

"Don't worry about it; I should have made sure you had everything you needed."

"So, what's on your agenda for today? I know you are so excited."

"More like extremely nervous. What if no one shows up?"

"Nicole, if your artwork in your gallery is anything like the artwork you have in your house, I'm sure you're going to have an excellent turn out. Did you advertise?"

"In every way possible," Nicole answered.

"Then you have nothing to worry about."

"Did Rashidi go to work with his father?" Nicole asked.

"Of course, he did. You would think they are Siamese twins."

Nicole laughed. "I knew it."

"They do look great together. He really wants to live here with you and Isaiah. I just can't let him go." Yvonne stated.

Nicole understood Yvonne. If she had the opportunity to give birth, she would never let her child go. "I truly understand. Girl, I need to get up. I have so much to do today. I have a hair appointment in thirty minutes. You want to go?" She offered.

"I would love too. I didn't come to Atlanta to stay cooped up. Isaiah said he booked me a room at the 'E' hotel, downtown. While we're out, maybe you drop me off, so I can check in. Maybe, I could do a little sight-seeing before the gallery opening."

"That's a great idea. Then Isaiah and Rashidi could pick you up, later on tonight."

"Ok, be ready in fifteen minutes." Yvonne rushed out of the room.

The shop phone rang. Isaiah and Rashidi were both under the hood of an older model SUV. His other mechanics were busy as well.

"Get the phone, please," Isaiah told his son.

Rashidi ran to the shop phone and answered it.

"Good morning, Complete Car Care. May I help you?"

"Is this my favorite grandson?" His grandmother asked.

"Good morning, Grandma. I'm your only grand-son," he smiled.

"So, just because you're my only grandson, doesn't mean you can't be my favorite."

"Whatever," he laughed. "I thought you were going to be here. Why didn't you come?"

"Trust me, baby, Grandma really wanted to be there. I haven't been feeling well, here lately."

"Are you ok?"

"I'm fine, baby, your grandmother is gettin' old. Trying to make that trip on the train or greyhound, I don't think I can handle that, right now."

"Then why don't you fly? It only takes an hour. You could have come with me and mom. Mom hates to fly."

"Your mother is there with you, in Atlanta, with your father and Nicole?" Gladys's heart began to race.

"Yes, we got here, last night."

"So, where is your mother staying?" She asked, concealing the strong dislike she felt for Rashidi's mother.

"We're staying with Dad and Nicole." Gladys Lucille Mathis began to panic, she knew what Yvonne was capable of.

"Sweetheart, please, put your father on the phone," She asked her grandson, trying not to sound alarmed.

"Are you ok, Grandma?" Rashidi could sense something was wrong.

"I'm fine, baby, just fine. Let me speak to your father."

"Ok, I love you. I hope you feel better."

"Thank you, baby, I love you, too." He put the receiver down and walked over to his father.

"Dad, Grandma is on the phone. I think something is wrong." Rashidi told his father.

Isaiah rushed to the phone.

"Hello, Mom, are you ok?" Isaiah asked, with his heart racing.

"I'm fine, are you ok? What the hell is that woman doing there? Is Yvonne staying in your house?"

"Yeah, Mom. Hold on, let me go into my office." He placed the call on hold and hung up the phone in the service garage.

He didn't want to talk in front of his son, about his son's mother.

"Rashidi do me a favor and help Harry with that tune up."

"Ok, Dad."

Isaiah walked into his office and retrieved the call. "Mom, don't get yourself all worked up over nothing. She only stayed in the house with us last night. I booked her a room at the 'E' hotel for the entire weekend. That is where she will stay while she's in Atlanta. The only reason she is here, is so I can convince her to allow Rashidi to live here with us, permanently."

"I don't like it one bit, Isaiah. I don't trust that woman, never have. It's a crying shame, that we live in the same state and that witch, won't let me spend time with my only grandson."

"Mom, relax, you'll only make yourself sick."

"I don't know why you never listen to me. I told you that woman was no good from the start."

"I know, you were right. Please, try and understand, I'm doing this for Rashidi."

"One of these days you are going to listen to me, Isaiah Jerome Mathis. I know your intentions are good, but you can't handle a fight with the devil, without the full armor of God."

"Yes, mom. I know. I have to go now. I have a lot of work to do. I love you."

"I love you, too, son. Good bye." She hung up the phone. Gladys knew what she had to do.

———

The women spent all morning together.

Nicole discovered that she really liked Yvonne and her uppity attitude. Yvonne had the eyes of a celebrity stylist, and personally selected what Nicole would wear tonight.

Yvonne on the other hand, figured that something about Nicole wasn't right. She couldn't pinpoint it, but her female intuition, had been triggered.

They went back to the house. They both entered the house from the garage.

Nicole's cell phone rang inside her purse. She quickly ran upstairs to her bedroom and threw her shopping bags on the bed. She retrieved her cell phone from her purse.

Yvonne went straight into the guest bathroom, upstairs.

"Hello?" Nicole answered.

"Hey, baby, you at home?" Isaiah asked.

"Yes, we just walked in the door." She replied, out of breath. "After we got our hair and nails done, I took Yvonne to the hotel, and she checked in. Then we went shopping. That's why I'm running so late. I don't have time to take her back to the hotel. Did your mother call you?"

"Yes, she called this morning. She went on and on about Yvonne being here. Rashidi told her that she flew here with him."

"Why does your mother dislike Yvonne so much?"

"She said she was no good for me. And to a certain extent, Mom was right."

"So, what are you guys up to?" Nicole asked.

"We are about to head home now. We had a busy day. You need anything?"

"I only need for you to be my side." Nicole smiled into the receiver.

"You got it. Rashidi wants to go with you. He wants to help you set up for tonight."

"Michelle called me earlier, while we were out, her babysitter cancelled. She wanted to know if Rashidi could watch the boys. Everyone we know is planning on coming to gallery grand opening tonight."

"Rashidi, your Aunt Michelle and Uncle Malik want to know if you wouldn't mind baby-sitting for a few of hours, tonight." Isaiah asked Rashidi.

"That's cool. Do I get to see the gallery first?" Nicole heard Rashidi ask.

"Tell him, that's fine, he can go with me now. I am leaving as soon as I get dressed. As a matter of fact, why don't you guys meet me at the gallery? I'll be there in thirty minutes."

"Sounds good." Isaiah said.

"Then you can drop Rashidi off at Michelle's house, come home, and get dressed. Hold on a second."

"How was your day with Yvonne?" Isaiah asked.

"Excellent, that woman really knows fashion. Wait until you see what she found for me to wear tonight." Nicole knocked on the bathroom door, "Yvonne, do you need to go back to your hotel room, to get ready for tonight?" She asked Yvonne.

"Not really, I have everything I need in my purse, as

long as I can borrow your flat iron. You get yourself ready." Yvonne said, through the door.

Isaiah heard Yvonne's response. "See you in thirty, love you." He said to Nicole.

"I love you, too. Tell Rashidi, I said, hello." Nicole responded.

"I will, bye." He hung up. She ended the call.

Yvonne poked her head out of the bathroom doorway.

"Isaiah and Rashidi are going to meet me at the gallery. Michelle wanted to know, if it would be ok for Rashidi to babysit her two sons, so they could attend the opening?" Nicole asked Yvonne.

"Who is Michelle?"

"Malik's wife."

"Malik actually found someone to marry his simple butt? I guess there really is someone for everybody." She laughed. "That doesn't say much for Michelle." She shrugged her shoulders, "I don't mind."

"I'm about to take a quick shower and get dressed. I can put on my make-up at the gallery." Nicole informed Yvonne.

"Isaiah is going to drop off Rashidi at Michelle's, and then he's going to come home to get dressed. You guys can come to the gallery together."

"That's fine. What time is it now?" Yvonne asked.

"It's four-thirty. I will see you later. Thank you for helping me with my outfit." Nicole said.

"You're welcome. See you at the gallery."

"Thank you." Nicole rushed into the bathroom.

Fifteen minutes later, Nicole was out the door with her cosmetic and garment bags in tow.

Yvonne decided it was time to find out about the real Nicole, Little Miss Perfect. Ain't no bitch this sweet and trusting. She crept into their bedroom, and headed for the medicine cabinet, carefully surveying its contents. Nicole is probably addicted to drugs, Yvonne hoped. Nothing was out of the ordinary. Yvonne took her time, and went through both nightstands, on both sides of the bed, careful not to disturb their contents. She found nothing.

She walked into their office, searching for anything to shatter their utopia. Making sure she inspected each and every file. Again, Yvonne found nothing. She knew that Isaiah would be home shortly. She decided she would wait for a more opportune time. She needed a drink. She headed downstairs to the kitchen. Nothing harsh, maybe a beer, she told herself. She opened the fridge and removed a Heineken. She began to open drawers in search of a bottle opener.

She opened the last drawer on the bottom and saw a manila envelope.

It was addressed to Isaiah and his mother, with page seventeen written on it.

She pulled out the magazine from the envelope, and read the title. She found page seventeen, and began to read, her eyes widened from the picture and the information. A crafty smile developed on her face. She placed the magazine back into the envelope and stuck it back into the drawer. She decided she would pass on the beer, and placed it back into the refrigerator. She needed a clear head to create her plan of attack. She heard someone at the front door.

Isaiah walked into the house.

"What up, Yvonne? I heard you two went shopping." Isaiah commented, as he walked into the kitchen.

He grabbed a bottle of water from the refrigerator.

"We did, had a great time." She smiled, seductively.

"I don't mean to rush you, but you need to get dressed. I have to make stop before we go to the gallery. I have a surprise for Nicole."

"Sure, no problem. No problem at all." I have a surprise for Nicole and you too, Yvonne smiled, wickedly.

Isaiah ran upstairs.

———

"I like her, Michelle. She seems like a wonderful person. We had a great time today, at the mall and at the salon."

"That's your problem, you like everybody. Nicole, she was downstairs damn-near naked, dripping water all over your house, in front of your man, with a towel on. I would have kicked her butt right back up those stairs, and then, put her ass out."

"You should have seen Rashidi. He was so embarrassed. He made her go back upstairs."

"What did Isaiah say?"

"It really pissed him off."

"Why is separated from her husband?" Michelle asked.

"She said they simply outgrew each other. He wanted more children and she refused."

"Whatever." Michelle said, pouring the last of the wine in the wine glasses. "How do I look?" Michelle put her hand on her hip and struck a pose.

"You look great, as usual." Nicole answered.

Michelle wore black and silver, asymmetrical blouse, revealing her left shoulder, with a full length black leather skirt and black, high-heeled, wedge boots. Her accessories were silver, with her jet black relaxed hair, flat-ironed to perfection.

"What about me, how do I look?" Nicole asked, pulling her hair all over one shoulder.

"I have to give it to Yvonne. You look like a star. That dress shows off all of your curves. I have to get me one of those. Did they come in my size?"

The butterfly dress was made from luxurious, brown printed jersey knit, which hung so elegantly from the body. It could be worn in dozens of ways.

Nicole twisted the long butterfly straps around and above her bosom and made the dress strapless.

The dress accentuated every curve of Nicole's hips and rear-end, as it elegantly cascaded to her feet. You could barely see her brown, jewel-encrusted, high-heeled sandals. Her earrings, bracelets and necklace matched her shoes, with her straightened hair, hanging below her breasts.

"They make these dresses in all sizes, for all body types." Nicole told Michelle.

"Was it expensive?"

"Not really."

"Girl, please, I know what your not really expensive, means. They could keep that dress."

"I can wear it so many different ways. It's like ten dresses in one."

"Anyway... let's have a quick prayer."

They held hands and bowed their heads.

"Dear Father God, we ask that you show up, and show out this evening. That you may show, Miss Nicole

Bennett, how gifted an artist she truly is. And how to use the gift that you gave her, to make all her dreams come true."

"Dear Father God, thank you for this incredible gift that you have graciously allowed me to borrow. I also want to thank you for the best friend that I could have ever imagined. Please, let Michelle know that she is truly appreciated."

"Amen." They said in unison. They hugged each other.

"Whatever happens tonight, Michelle, I want you to know that I really love you. I truly appreciate your friendship. Thank you sharing this special evening with me."

"Oh, girl, I love you, too. Now let's remove the curtains, and turn on the music. Girl, its show time." Michelle said, excitedly.

NINE

As they removed the curtains from the windows and front door, they were surprised at the number of people waiting to enter the gallery.

Michelle unlocked the front doors and held it open for the awaiting guests.

"Hello, and welcome to KNB Art Gallery. We are serving alcohol. Please have your identification ready, thank you. The complimentary greeting cards, are in the large basket, on the wine table, in the center of the gallery."

"Are you the artist?" One of the customers asked.

"No, ma'am, she is," Michelle answered, presenting Nicole like one of the Price-is-Right girls.

"Good evening, ladies and gentlemen, I am Nicole

Bennett, welcome to KNB art gallery. KNB stands for Kyla Nicole Bennett; she was my deceased sister, who was killed last month by a drunk driver. She was the first person who believed in my artistic abilities. Thank you for coming. Please, have a glass of wine or champagne, and enjoy the art."

A mature lady approached Nicole and introduced herself. "Hello, my name is Ester Robinson."

"Pleased to meet you, Ester, I'm Nicole, welcome to KNB."

"I was wondering, have you drawn any portraits of the President?"

"I sure did, right over here." She led the impeccably dressed lady to the Celebrity section. "I started his piece right before the primaries. I completed it before he received the nomination. I wanted to capture a piece of him that portrayed his spiritual side." Nicole explained.

"I love it." The lady looked at the price. "Is this the original. I'll take it.?"

Nicole removed the beautifully framed limited-edition print from the gallery wall.

"No, ma'am. The original is not for sale. We are trying to get it to the President."

"Good luck to you. You are very talented."

"Thank you very much. I will leave this behind the register. You can purchase it, on your way out. Please, help yourself to a glass of wine or champagne, and a complimentary greeting card."

"I will. Thank you." Mrs. Robinson started to walk away.

"Excuse me, is that piece for sale?" A gentleman asked Nicole.

Ester stopped and turned around.

"I'm sorry, she just..." Nicole was interrupted as Ester returned and took the piece from Nicole hands.

"If you don't mind, I'll take it with me." Ester stated.

"Yes, ma'am."

"Do you have more portraits of the President in a frame?"

"I sure do. I also have a limited-edition print without the frame."

"I want it exactly like hers."

"Yes Sir, coming right up." Nicole responded cheerfully.

She walked back into her office and pulled two framed portraits of the President from her overstock inventory.

She walked back into the gallery as she was approached by adoring supporters.

"Thank you. Thank you very much for coming out and showing your support. I really appreciate it. If you will excuse me, I'll be right back." She hung one of the framed pictures in the empty spot on the wall.

She spotted the gentleman customer gazing at the other art in a different section. "Here you go, Sir," Nicole said, extending the framed picture to him.

"I love this one, too," he said, admiring 'Ghetto Love'- a beautiful woman, braiding a handsome man's hair, in Central Park. "I like how you captured the emotion on the woman's face."

"Yes, this is one of my personal favorites." Nicole replied.

"The black and white, double matting really makes the art stand out. This piece is speaking to me. Your ability to capture detail is extraordinary. This has to be the original. I prefer to collect originals."

"You are correct."

"I'll take it. I must have *Ghetto Love*."

"Yes Sir," Nicole beamed with pride, controlling her excitement, as she removed the original from the wall.

The same customer looked at the price of the framed portrait of the President. "I assume this piece is a framed print."

"Yes, Sir."

"I will take both. This one of the President is incredible. It will fit in nicely in my art collection. People will assume that it's the original."

"Thank you."

"How much is the original of the president?"

"I'm sorry the original is not for sale. We are working to get the original to the President."

"I understand. If you need my help, I have several influential connections. By the way, my name is Stan Murphy. Here's my card."

"It is very nice to meet you, Mr. Murphy." His business card stated that he was a Sports Attorney.

"Please, call me Stan."

Nicole looked around the crowded gallery for Michelle.

Michelle had her hands full with several customers of her own. "Ok, Stan, if you will follow me to the register; I will check you out."

He took one of the framed pieces from her and followed her to the register.

"You definitely have a gift."

"Thank you, Stan. I sincerely appreciate your support."

"I appreciate your gift. My daughter is an artist. Hopefully, when she sees your art, it will inspire her to get serious"

"Make sure you tell her, that practice, makes perfect. The more she draws, the better she will get."

"Excuse me; did he just buy that piece?" Another

sharply dressed man asked Nicole, holding a glass of wine.

He was referring to 'Ghetto Love'.

"Yes, I did, it's the original." Stan boasted.

"Do you have a print of that in a frame?"

"I do. If you will give me a minute to finish with Mr. Murphy, I will be happy to get it for you."

"Sure, take your time." The gentleman walked away.

"Looks like you're going to have a successful grand opening." Stan said.

"This is unbelievable." *Where is Isaiah? I wanted him to be a part of the first sale.*

"A woman as beautiful and as talented as yourself, I'm sure you have husband or boyfriend." Stan noticed the sizeable rock on Nicole's hand.

"I do, he's on the way."

"You make sure you tell him, he's lucky man."

"I will."She smiled.

"What does KNB stand for?"

"They are my sister's initials. She died a few weeks ago, so I dedicated my art gallery to her memory." She finished her transaction with the customer and offered him assistance to his automobile with his purchases.

"No, I can handle this," Stan assured her. "Your public awaits you. Thank you for sharing your gift. I'm sure this is only the beginning for you. Congratulations. I will definitely keep in touch, I know people."

"Thank you for your support, Mr. Murphy. Have a great evening."

"You're welcome, Nicole. I'll see you again." He walked out of the door. Michelle walked up to the register followed by several customers carrying framed and unframed artwork.

"Girl, this is crazy," Michelle whispered to Nicole.

"Tell me about it."

"Are you going to the office?" Michelle asked.

"Yes, what did you need?"

"Grab me, 'In Flight'-an agile ballerina captured in mid-air. I also need another 'Elevation'-a male dancer supporting a female ballerina. I sold both originals. This is my boss and his wife, David and Cathy Clarke, at Universal and these are some of my co-workers. This is the artist, Nicole Bennett." Michelle introduced them.

They swarmed around Nicole, complimenting her artistic ability.

She politely thanked them individually for their support and answered each of their questions regarding her work. Then she politely excused herself and invited them to come back again.

She took a deep breath as she walked into her office and closed the door. She fell to her knees, held up her outstretched hands, and thanked GOD openly, for the incredible life that she had been blessed with. She remembered all the heartache and suffering she had to endure to make it to this day. She fought back tears of joy as gratefulness consumed her. She stood back up, and hastily selected the framed art she needed from overstock.

Isaiah walked into her office followed by Yvonne.

"Congratulations, it's all the way up, out there." Isaiah stated proudly.

Nicole leaned the framed pictures against her desk and rushed into Isaiah's embrace.

They kissed passionately.

"They are buying up everything." Yvonne commented, suddenly feeling nauseous, witnessing Isaiah kiss Nicole.

"This is unbelievable, and I owe it all to you." Nicole said, kissing Isaiah again.

"I can't take the credit for the art you create. You do the same thing for me at Complete Car Care. You support and believe in me." He smiled.

"The gallery was all your idea. I love you so much, Isaiah."

"That woman out there said to hurry up with the art." Yvonne pointed out, jealous of the way Isaiah was holding Nicole, remembering the times when he held her. It made her sick to her stomach to know that Isaiah was now involved with another man. She knew she had the power to cure Isaiah's homosexuality.

"I'll get the art. You go out there and shine." Isaiah said to Nicole. Isaiah picked up the art as they all walked out of the office. He locked the door and put the keys in his pocket.

"You can hang those pieces on the empty spaces on the right side of the wall." Nicole said to Isaiah.

Yvonne took Nicole by the arm and escorted her to the drawing of Rashidi.

"Do you remember what you said? This one, the original is mine, right?" Yvonne asked, referring to the original drawing of Rashidi, on the tripod. "I have never known female artists to do this type of art. Normally, men do this type of art." Yvonne stated.

"Really? I know several female portrait artists." Nicole found Yvonne's remark to be odd, but she had no time to worry about it now. She wanted to help Isaiah, to show him where to place the framed art.

Yeah, right, Yvonne thought. "Girl, you have a gift." She gave Nicole a fake smile.

"Thank you for coming Yvonne, and for bringing Rashidi," Nicole excused herself.

With Nicole's instruction, Isaiah hung the art in their proper places.

Isaiah embraced Nicole from behind, wrapping his arms around her waist, kissing her on the neck.

Nicole reached her arms up and caressed Isaiah's bald head.

Nicole's parents, William and Elizabeth Bennett, and Gregory Thompson, her brother in-law, entered the gallery.

Gregory was holding her nephew, Jonathan.

"Surprise." Isaiah whispered in Nicole's ear.

Nicole hands immediately crossed over her chest. She was speechless as tears welled in the corners of her eyes. She spun around and hugged Isaiah.

"Thank you, Isaiah." Nicole cried.

As soon as Gregory set Jonathan down, Jonathan ran to Nicole.

She bent down and scooped him up, off his feet.

"Hi, little man, how are you?" She kissed him on the cheek. "It's so nice to see you, again."

"Hi, Aunty Nicole, we came to see you." Jonathan said to Nicole.

"Oh my God, I'm so happy to see you. I'm so glad you're here." Nicole walked over to her family and kissed them all on the cheek as tears flowed from her eyes. "Thank you so much for coming." She cried as she hugged her mother.

Elizabeth was crying, too.

"We wouldn't have missed it for the world," William smiled, as he touched Nicole's shoulder. "Your art is amazing."

"You look so beautiful." Elizabeth said.

"You are so talented," Gregory added. "This is really incredible."

"Thank you, Gregory. You look beautiful, too, Mom." Nicole said to her mother as they hugged again.

"I had no idea that you were this talented. Your talent comes from my side of the family. I'm so proud of you." Her father boasted.

"Thank you."

Her father handed her a large bouquet of red roses in an exquisite golden vase. "Congratulations, these are for you."

Nicole set Jonathan down on the gallery carpet.

"Thank you." She graciously accepted the beautiful floral arrangement.

Her mother handed her a large pink gift bag, decorated with various shades of pink tissue paper.

"Gregory transferred all of your sister's home videos to DVD. He has included footage from her sixth grade graduation, her wedding, holding her son for the first time, and everything in between."

She hugged Gregory. "Wow, thank you Gregory, that is so sweet. I can't wait to watch them. Thank you all.

Let me put these in my office. Isaiah and I will show you around."

Isaiah opened the office door for her and relocked it.

They both returned to her parents.

"I love the name of the gallery. Your sister would be so proud of you." Her father stated.

"She will never be forgotten." Nicole responded as they walked to the back of the gallery.

Isaiah directed their attention to the drawing Nicole drew of Kyla.

Her mother cried openly.

Nicole cradled her nephew in her arms. "So how do you like Atlanta?" She asked her nephew.

"I like it, it's cold." Jonathan answered. "I like your art. You draw good."

"Well, thank you, nephew." She kissed him on the cheek again, happy to hold a piece of her sister.

"That is the most beautiful picture I have ever seen. Your sister was a work of art." Her father said.

"It yours, this is the original." Isaiah navigated himself behind the counter, where Michelle was busy helping customers. He removed the exquisitely framed piece from the wall and handed it to her father.

"Thank you." Her parents said in unison.

"Gregory, we have a framed reproduction at the house, if you want it." Isaiah offered.

"I would love that."

William held it up for his grandson to see. "You know that this is your mother, when she was a little girl," William said.

"Mommie is pretty."

"Yes, she is," Nicole agreed.

"Is that the greatest over there?" William said, referring to the drawing of Muhammad Ali. "I have to have it. It will be the centerpiece of my sports room."

"You can have any piece you want, William. This is our gift to you for making this evening special for Nicole." Isaiah said.

"This is a business, Isaiah. I can buy what I want, just like everybody else." William said sternly.

"He's right, Isaiah, we are here to support you and my daughter." Elizabeth interjected, wiping the tears from her eyes.

Nicole took her mother's hand and offered an introduction, "I'm sorry, Yvonne, these are my parents, Mr. and Mrs. William Bennett, and my brother-in-law, Gregory Thompson, and my nephew, Jonathan Thompson, and this is Yvonne Jones, Isaiah's son's mother."

"We've already been introduced. We picked them up from the hotel. I need a glass of wine." Yvonne replied.

"I would like a glass of wine, too. I will go with Yvonne," Elizabeth said.

"I'm going to look around, I'll take Jonathan," Gregory said.

Jonathan was reluctant to leave his aunt's arms.

"I'll go with you, son." His father-in-law joined him. Yvonne had heard enough and walked away.

"Nicole." Michelle said, flagging Nicole to come join her at the register.

"Go ahead, we're going to look around." Her mother said.

"Wait, please. I want you to meet my best friend, Michelle." Nicole begged.

She introduced her family and Yvonne to Michelle. They all exchanged pleasantries.

"We can see that you are busy. We are going to look around." Her father said.

"Ok, I will see you later." Her family walked away with Isaiah.

"Girl, I have been on this register non-stop, since I jumped on it. There is a lot of money in here. The art bins, and greeting card racks, need replenishing."

"I will replenish the art. Do you think we should have Isaiah watch the register?" Nicole asked.

"Isaiah needs to remove some of this cash and lock it in your office; the cash drawer is almost full." Michelle informed Nicole.

"That's a good idea." Nicole agreed.

Malik walked in the gallery, dressed in a suit and tie. He saw his wife with Nicole, in the rear of the gallery and approached them.

"Damn baby, you look delicious." Malik kissed his wife.

"Thank you, Pooh-Pooh, you are looking good, too. How are the kids?"

"They are fine. My man Rashidi is holding it down. You look great, Nicole." Malik kissed Nicole on the cheek. "Congratulations, it's packed up in here. How's business, tonight?"

"Thank you for coming, Malik. Tonight, has exceeded our expectations."

"You know Michelle and I, got you and Isaiah's back."

"Nicole, before you run off again, please send Isaiah over here to put some more art in the bins and greeting card racks. And don't forget the empty spaces on the wall." Michelle instructed. Nicole noticed Isaiah giving her parents the grand tour of the gallery. She walked over to him and sent Isaiah over to Michelle.

"What up, dog?!" Isaiah spotted Malik standing next to his wife. They shook hands and hugged simultaneously. "Welcome to KNB."

"Man, this is real nice. Nicole hooked it up in here."

"You know it. My girl got skills."

"Isaiah, it's over two thousand dollars of cash in here." Michelle interrupted. "You need to take some of this cash and lock it Nicole's office."

"Count out the majority and put it in the bag. Make sure you leave yourself enough change." Isaiah said.

Michelle removed the excess cash, the credit cards receipts, and placed them into a locking drop bag. She handed the bag to Isaiah. "I see Nicole over there with customers. When you go into the office, pull out all of the big boxes, against the wall. Those are back stock of packaged prints. The greeting card back stock is organized on the shelves. Restock the art bins and greeting card racks. And put some of the framed art in the empty spaces on the wall." Michelle instructed.

He and Malik walked towards Nicole's office.

Yvonne intercepts them.

"Well, well, well, Mr. Malik, look at you. I have to give it to you, you are looking good. I haven't seen you since high school, how have you been?"

"Hey, Yvonne, how you doing?" Malik tried to disguise the dislike he felt for her. She nearly ended his and Isaiah's friendship, while they attended high school.

"I'm fine, thank you for asking. Who would have thought that a goofy, gangly, ugly duckling, could transform into a strapping, tower of masculinity? Very nice. I've already had the pleasure of being introduced to your beautiful, and extremely, healthy wife." Yvonne blew out her cheeks for emphasis. Before Malik could respond, Isaiah pulled him away, into Nicole's office.

"I never did like that bitch. How the hell do you put up with her?" Malik questioned.

"Hopefully, it won't be for much longer." Isaiah answered.

"How do Nicole and Yvonne get along?"

"Nicole thinks she's cool. I just want my son."

"Good luck with that, man. She's still a bitch."

Isaiah locked the bag in bottom drawer of the desk.

Everything in Nicole's office was so neat, and plainly organized, that they found the prints, greeting cards, and framed art.

They locked the office, took all the back stock, and put them into the nearly empty bins and greeting card racks. They also placed the framed art in the empty spaces on the walls.

"I have to make another run, you wanna roll with me?" Isaiah asked Malik.

"Let me see if Michelle needs anything."

Malik walked up to the register; Isaiah handed Nicole's office keys to Michelle. "Hey baby, you need anything? I'm going to run with Isaiah."

"Pooh-Pooh, we need you here. We need more wine and champagne from the fridge. Did you guys replenish the bins and greeting card racks?" Michelle handed the office keys to her husband.

"The bins and greeting card racks are full." Isaiah smiled. "People are buying up everything."

"Hey Isaiah, you going to have roll solo, they need my help." Malik said.

"All right, be back in twenty."

Yvonne intercepted Isaiah, before he walked out of the door.

Malik removed his sports coat.

"Where are you going now?" Yvonne asked Isaiah.

"I have another surprise for Nicole."

"Can I go for the ride?"

"Sure, I guess. Why did you say that fucked-up shit to Malik, about his wife?"

"You know, I was only kidding." Yvonne lied as they were walking out of the gallery.

They bumped into Winston Horne, the man from the airport as they were walking toward Isaiah's SUV.

"Hello, Yvonne." Winston said.

"Hello, man from the airport. I see you made it." Yvonne rolled her eyes.

"How are you doing? Isaiah Mathis." Isaiah said, extending his hand, introducing himself.

"Nice to meet you, Winston Horne."

They shook hands.

"Yvonne, why don't you give Mr. Horne, the grand tour of the gallery? I'll be right back."

Before Yvonne could respond, Isaiah started jogging towards the SUV.

———

Nicole was busy tending to customers. Her current customer had ten prints, trying to figure out which ones were imperative to add to her art collection.

Someone tapped her on the shoulder, and she turned around.

"Good evening, Artist, how you been?" Chuck Wilson, the mechanic asked, with his arms outstretched, awaiting a hug.

"Hello, Mr. Wilson, how are you?" She hugged him. "I'm doing great. Thank you for coming. Where is your wife, Pauline?"

"She is over there looking thru the bins; she really likes the one of the President."

"I have an idea; I have one left in a frame." Nicole whispered in Chuck's ear. "I will sell it to Pauline for fifty dollars. After all, you two were my first customers."

"She'll love that."

Nicole excused herself from her customer and removed the portrait from the wall.

They walked over to Pauline.

"Hello, Pauline, how are you? Thank you for coming." Nicole hugged Pauline.

"Hello Nicole, Honey-childchild, your work is fabulous. You remember the portraits you drew of me and my husband, and the children?"

Nicole nodded her head in agreement.

"Every time them children of mine come to the house, they trying to take my artwork," Pauline laughed. "I don't play when it comes to my artwork. I love this print of the President."

"Baby, look," her husband said, holding up the framed picture of the President. "Nicole said we could have it for fifty bucks." He whispered in her ear.

"Thank you, Nicole." Pauline hugged her again.

"Thank you for being here and showing me love. Enjoy."

"We will. Thank you. By the way, where is Isaiah?" Chuck asked.

Nicole looked around. "You know what, Mr. Wilson, that's a good question. He was just here a second ago."

"Make sure you tell him that we came through."

"I sure will." Nicole said.

Pauline continued shopping.

Nicole walked up behind her parents. "So, what do you think?"

They both turned around and hugged her.

"Your work is incredible. Who would have thought that your little cartoon characters would turn into this?" Her mother stated.

"We are so proud of you." They said in unison.

"When you told us in San Diego that you were and artist, I had no idea, that you possessed this level of talent. We are going to purchase at least six originals. We're going to hang them in the living room. Our living room is going to become a small KNB gallery." Her father added proudly.

"That is so sweet, thank you." Nicole hugged her parents.

"No, thank you." Her father said, as he looked over Nicole's shoulder.

William focused his attention to the gallery entrance. "Oh my God, is that Brock Bass?"

Nicole turned around as the local television cameras entered the gallery, followed behind Brock Bass, and his entourage.

With the help of his personal security men, they made their way through the crowd, and approached Nicole.

She recognized Deborah Johnson, a reporter from the Weekend Report, Evening news.

"Five, Four, Three, Two, One. Good evening, ladies and gentlemen, we are here, live, at KNB Art Gallery, located at 1576 Turner Hill Rd in Lithonia. I am with the two-time, Professional Football Championship MVP, recent Hall-of-Famer, and Celebrity Sports Bar Mogul, Brock Bass. Mr. Bass is here to make a special announcement to the owner of KNB Art Gallery, Nicole Bennett." Deborah handed the microphone to Brock.

"Miss Bennett, on behalf of B.B. Sports Bars, Restaurants and Casino; I would like to offer you an exclusive contract as the official artist of my Sports Bars and Casino." Brock said. Brock aimed the microphone at her mouth, awaiting Nicole's response.

Nicole was speechless and visibly angry.

Michelle made her way through the crowd, and stood next to Nicole, glaring angrily at Brock.

Malik stood on the other side of Nicole as he dialed Isaiah on his cell phone.

"Cut! Obviously, she is at a loss for words. Why don't you guys get some shots of her artwork, and inter-view a few people, regarding her artwork. Then we'll come back to get her response." He handed the micro-phone back to Deborah, the news reporter.

Brock leaned in close to Nicole, and whispered in her

ear, "You look great. Did your friend receive my manila envelopes?"

Nicole was dumbfounded.

"B.B, my all-time favorite quarterback, how the hell are you? I'm your biggest fan!" William Bennett yelled, excitedly.

All the men in the gallery rushed Brock.

Michelle took Nicole by the hand and led her into the office.

Malik went back to the register to help customers.

"I knew it, I knew it. I told you that asshole was going to show up!" Michelle shouted as she sat on Nicole's desk and unzipped her boots. "He was behind that shit, the whole time." She kicked off her boots and removed her earrings. She pulled her hair back into a ponytail. "Now, I'm about to show you, how Michelle really gets down! Girl, bye!" Michelle started stretching and doing exercise lunges. Then she started shadow boxing, releasing shorts breaths with each imaginary punch.

"Michelle, what am I going to do?" Nicole asked in shock.

"I can't wait until Isaiah gets back. We are going to tear BB's ass up!"

Nicole panicked, she realized that she needed to get

rid of Brock, before Isaiah returned and all hell broke loose. "I'll be right back."

"Wait, where are you going?" Michelle grabbed Nicole by the wrist.

"I've got to get BB out of here."

"All the pain he's caused you, why would you care?"

"I have worked far too hard, to stand and watch, as our gallery gets destroyed. Michelle, did you hear what BB said? He has just offered me the job of my dreams. Think of the exposure my art would receive. The least I could do is hear him out."

"How do think Isaiah will feel about you working with Brock Bass?"

"Hopefully, Isaiah will understand, *this* is business. This was all his idea. B.B. could take my art to whole new level. Think of the exposure the art will receive. Isn't this the reason we opened the gallery in the first place?"

"Haven't you noticed? You're doing quite well without Brock. You don't need him."

"You're right. I don't need him, but I do need the gallery. If I don't get BB out of here, before Isaiah returns, we won't have a gallery. Please, let me get BB out of here."

"Whatever...I'll come with you." As soon as they exited they locked up the office.

Deborah approached them, "Hello, and congratulations, Miss Bennett. It is a pleasure to meet you. Your artwork is phenomenal. Can I get a quick interview?"

"Of course, can I please talk to BB, first?"

"Sure, I'll look around." Michelle noticed her husband struggling with the register. She took over for him.

Nicole walked up to Brock, surrounded by his fans, and tapped him on the shoulder. "Excuse me, can I talk to you in private, please?"

"I thought you'd never ask." Brock excused himself from his adoring fans, as his personal security escorted them through the crowd. "Let's go out front. It's a mad house in here."

They stepped outside, to the end of the strip mall, monitored by his security.

"It seems as though you're having an excellent gallery opening. You're welcome. You can thank me, later." He winked at Nicole. "My friends and associates, are texting me like crazy, about your artwork."

"What did you have to do with my gallery opening?" She asked.

"Everything, don't you know who I am? I know everybody, and everybody knows me. Where do you think all these people came from?" Brock answered.

"Are you serious?" Nicole laughed. She realized who she was talking to, Mr. Arrogant. "Whatever. Why would you send those envelopes to Isaiah and his mother? Isaiah nearly killed me."

"It was never my intention to compromise your life. My only desire was to end your relationship with him. Nicole, let me share a little something with you. A great businessman recognizes a potential gold mine. When I saw your early drawings, years ago, I could see your profitability. I needed you to master your craft. You were an extremely costly investment. Do you honestly think that I would let my investment simply run away, and become another man's gain? I don't think so. If the manila envelopes didn't get the job done, I was willing to execute more extreme measures. I sincerely apologize that you had to get hurt in the process."

"I hate to burst your bubble, but it didn't work. All I was, was an investment to you." Nicole asked, offended.

"No, you also performed superior, oral copulation." BB smiled.

"Why would you do that to me? How did you find me?" Nicole asked, becoming angrier by the second.

"I traced you from your car. You sold it here, and I employed a very expensive private investigator, to do the rest."

"You attempted to destroy my life."

"How could you possibly have a life, without me in it, Nicole? Didn't we have some good times?" He stroked her cheek. She pushed his hand away from her face.

"Did it ever occur to you, that I love him? And that he loves me?"

"Honestly, do you really think, a transsexual, could seriously be transformed into a mother and a wife? How can a black, back-woods, southern mechanic, offer you the lifestyle that I could provide for you? When I initially met you, I was extremely unhappy with my personal life, which should have explained my need for prostitutes. Financially, I was doing well, but personally, I was suffering. I was forced into a marriage with a woman that I couldn't stand, which led to my alcoholism. I have changed my life in numerous ways. I am happily divorced and completely single. I am no longer a bitter, alcoholic."

"So, you're saying that you are willing to be seen with me publicly, without your assistant?"

"I'm here now without Dennis, aren't I?"

"And you are willing to jeopardize your businesses and career, for an African American, transgendered, female?"

"I am willing to take a chance with you, but if your sexuality was made public, I would terminate the contract. I would publicly deny that I knew your true identity."

"Are you willing to make me your wife?"

"Come on now, you can't be serious? I'm not ready for commitment, let alone marriage again. You couldn't legally marry in Georgia anyway. I am offering you the job of a lifetime, in addition to prolonging our special friendship."

"Think about me, Isaiah is offering me the life that I have always dreamed of, as a wife and step-mother."

"The job offer is real. I will provide you a list of the sports celebrities scheduled to appear at my restaurants and casino. They are booked months in advance, which would give you plenty of time to create their portraits. I want it similar to the Brown Derby in Old Hollywood, instead of actors, I want sports celebrities. Your art will be the focal point of the restaurants, and casino, along with the sports memorabilia. We're going to have them sign the original, frame them and hang them up. Then we will present the celebrity with a framed reproduction of the original. You will be paid handsomely for your artistic renderings; a way for my investment to pay off for both of us. This is also my way of apologizing for every-thing I put you through, having to endure dealing with the old me."

"I sincerely appreciate your business offer, but I need some time to think it over. I need to ask you a favor. Isaiah will be here any moment. Will you please leave, and I will call as soon as I get a chance. I will need some time to convince Isaiah of your business arrangement. And in response to your special friendship offer, there is no chance of a sexual relationship between us, ever."

"I believe you have forgotten with whom you are dealing. I'm in control. We've never had a business relationship without sex. I personally created you, and demand the privilege to experience you, whenever I, desire. I will leave, simple because I don't want to see your insignificant, little friend get hurt. Be a good little girl and go back inside and give them an interview. Tell them we met at an art festival, or something like that, and I will contact you later." Brock left Nicole standing there.

He was escorted to his SUV by his security team and left.

Nicole walked back into the gallery. Everyone was shaking her hand, hugging her, and congratulating her.

Michelle and Malik frowned at her, disapprovingly.

Deborah approached her. "Are you ready for your interview, Miss Bennett? Don't worry, BB, provided me with a list of short, simple questions; nothing too personal, or revealing."

"Yes, ma'am." Nicole remembered what Brock told her to say. She saw her parents in the crowd and asked her father for the drawing of Kyla.

"Michael, bring the camera. I need you to set it up right here, please." Deborah instructed.

The small crew set up the tripod and the mobile lighting.

"We're ready." Michael, the camera man said.

"Five, four, three, two, one. Good evening, ladies and gentlemen, we are here live, at KNB Art Gallery on Turner Hill Rd, with the owner, and artist, Nicole Bennett. Who minutes ago, discovered that she was chosen as the contract artist for B.B. Sports Grills, and Casino. What does the name of the gallery KNB stand for Miss Bennett?"

"Those are my deceased sister's initials. This is her picture." Nicole held up the drawing.

"She is adorable. Your artwork looks like a photograph. This is a drawing?"

"Yes, ma'am."

"What is your medium of choice?"

"Charcoal, and sometimes, I will add pastels, for a pop of color."

"Your ability to capture details is amazing. Please, get a close-up, so the viewers can see the intricate details and depth of her work. How did Mr. Bass, become familiar with your work?"

"Mr. Bass became familiar with my work, from an art show here in Atlanta. I am so humbled and honored, to be offered an opportunity to be part of B.B. Sports Bars and Casinos. I sincerely thank Mr. Bass, for this incredible opportunity."

"Do you do commissioned art?"

"Of course, I draw family portraits, animals, landscapes. I can draw anything."

"Well, congratulations and we wish you continued success. We look forward to seeing more of your amazing artwork. For you serious art collectors, I highly recommend KNB Art gallery, located at 1576 Turner Hill Rd. KNB has a wide of array of artistic renderings, ranging from celebrities, to spiritual, and modern ballet. I am Deborah Johnson, with WNSB news. Goodnight. Cut! Ok you guys, that's a wrap." She handed the microphone to one of her people.

"Thank you very much, Miss Johnson, for this incredible opportunity. That interview will bring good exposure to the gallery."

"You're welcome. You really should thank Mr. Bass, this was all his idea. I love that framed portrait of the young lady holding the cross. That would go great in my daughter's bedroom."

"That piece is titled, *HOLD ON*."

"I will take the original."

"Wow, thank you very much; I sincerely appreciate

your support." Nicole removed the picture from the wall. "Michelle will ring you up, right over here."

"I can now say that I have a Nicole Bennett original, before she became famous. It was a pleasure meeting you, I'm sure we'll see each other again." Deborah Johnson stated.

"Thank you, I look forward to it." Nicole responded.

Deborah hugged Nicole.

Michelle and Malik frowned at her disapprovingly.

Her parents walked up to her from behind and hugged her.

"We are so proud of you Nicole. Your gallery is a great success."

"I didn't know Brock Bass is familiar with your artwork. How did you meet him?" Her father asked, extremely impressed.

"I met him at an art festival in Atlanta." She lied to them.

"Like us, he wants to showcase your gift. Your sister would be so proud of you." Her mother added.

"Thank you, that means so much to me." Nicole smiled.

Isaiah entered the gallery, without his suit coat and tie, searching for Brock.

On his right side, stood Peppa, her surrogate mother, with her hand in her purse, prepared for war. Brian, her friend that rescued her in Alabama, entered behind them.

"Peppa!!! Brian!!!" Nicole ran up to Peppa, and embraced her tightly. She did the same to Brian.

"Hi, baby. Where is he?" Peppa asked, angrily.

"Hello, Nicole, you look great." Brian exclaimed.

"Thank you, Brian. Brock has left already." Nicole informed Isaiah and Peppa.

"This is your artwork? You are incredible." Brian stated, looking around the gallery.

"Thank you. Thank you so much for coming. Momma, you would not believe the sales we've had tonight, through the roof. I want to introduce you to someone." Nicole said to Peppa.

She escorted Peppa and Brian, to her parents, who were being congratulated by Nicole's adoring supporters.

"Excuse me, everybody I want to introduce you to my surrogate mother, Peppa Bingham, and my dear friend, Brian Cullens. Brian rescued me in Alabama." They all exchanged pleasantries.

She then escorted Peppa and Brian to Michelle and Malik. "Michelle and Malik, this is Peppa Bingham, my surrogate mother, you know her from our phone calls."

"It is so nice to finally meet you in person. Welcome

to Atlanta," Michelle said as she came from behind the counter and hugged Peppa.

"Hello, how you doing?" Malik said, as he shook Peppa's hand, politely.

"I'm fine, thank you, and yourself?" Peppa answered.

"No complaints." Malik responded.

"Miss Peppa, after this is over, we need to have a long conversation with your child. Nicole needs help." Michelle interjected.

"You're just figuring that out now?" Peppa responded as they laughed.

Nicole continued the introductions. "Anyway, Michelle, this is Brian Cullens. Brian, you already met Malik, when he picked up my car."

Nicole hugged Brian again. "I can't believe that you're here."

"Hello, Brian. I really appreciate what you did for Nicole. Thank you." Michelle embraced Brian, warmly. "Welcome to the family."

"Thank you, It was no problem at all, she's a very talented lady." Brian replied.

"What up, man? How you been?" Malik asked Brian, as he shook his hand.

"Good, thank you."

"I'm going to look at the art," Peppa exclaimed.

"I'm going to join her, please excuse us." Brian added

as he and Peppa walked away arm in arm. Nicole walked up to Isaiah, who was visibly upset.

"Isaiah, this has been one of the greatest days of my life. I owe it all to you." Nicole tried to kiss him on the lips, and Isaiah turned away.

"Why the hell did you let BB leave, before I got here? Michelle said, you didn't let her confront him, either. Did you walk outside with him? What was that shit about?" Isaiah questioned Nicole, angrily.

"It wasn't like we could talk in here, with all these people, and television crew. Brock apologized to me, and offered me a job that I can't refuse." Nicole explained.

"What do you mean a job, you can't refuse? You are not going to have anything to do with Brock Bass. I don't care what he offered you."

"Isaiah, do you hear what you're saying? Remember, this was all your idea. Brock is offering us the opportunity of a lifetime."

"We don't need B.B for anything. You are going to be successful because of what God gave you. B.B has nothing to do with it."

"Can't we even discuss it?"

"There is nothing to discuss, period." Isaiah walked out of the gallery.

Yvonne noticed the disagreement and followed Isaiah out of the gallery.

"Wow, you two have made enough money tonight for early retirement." Yvonne laughed as she approached Isaiah. "Are you alright? I could always tell when you're upset." She touched his arm.

He pulled away.

"I'm alright. I can't believe this shit. She tried to protect him."

"What? She tried to protect who?" Yvonne asked, even though she's seen Nicole with BB and had overheard part of their conversation on the sidewalk.

Nicole suddenly exited the gallery and approached them.

"Isaiah, can I please talk to you for a minute?" Nicole asked.

"I ain't got nothing to say. We will talk when we get home. Are your parents ready to go back to the hotel? It's ten after nine. Tell them, I'm waiting in the truck." Isaiah started to walk away.

"I guess, I'll meet you at home." Nicole called out.

"I have to pick up Rashidi, I'll meet you at Maliks.'" He walked away, towards the truck in the parking lot.

Nicole watched Isaiah walk away.

Yvonne scooted closer to Nicole, "Girl, trust me, he'll be ok. He used to do the same thing to me. I'll talk to him for you. You remember that guy you invited from the airport, Winston Horne. He bought two pieces tonight. He wanted to thank you personally, but you were so busy with customers and the news crew."

"That is so nice, are you going to see him again?" Nicole asked.

"I don't think so, he's not my type. You go back inside; everything will be fine. I will get Isaiah to calm down."

"Thank you, Yvonne." Nicole hugged her.

No, thank you, stupid bitch. Thank you for making it so easy to take my man back.

What have I done? Nicole thought to herself. All my friends, and my fiancé, are upset with me. This may prove to be the worst day of my life. She took a deep breath and walked back inside the gallery.

TEN

Nicole entered the gallery and noticed that the background music had been turned off.

Michelle approached her at the door. "It's time to close up shop. I just turned the music off. You need to let everyone know that we are closing."

"Ok." Nicole cleared her throat and took a deep breath. "Excuse me, everyone, may I have your attention please? I sincerely want to thank each and every one of you, from the bottom of my heart, for making this evening, one that I will never forget. Unfortunately, it's after nine o'clock, and we have to close. We are closed for the next three days. We re-open Tuesday. Please, keep in mind, the normal gallery hours are Tuesday thru Saturday, from noon to eight pm, the gallery is closed on Sunday and Mondays. Again, I thank you all for the love and support. Enjoy the rest of your evening." Nicole spoke loud and clear.

The audience applauded her.

Nicole bowed gracefully.

The guests all made sure to greet her, before they left the gallery with their purchases.

Her parents walked up to her.

"We are so happy for you." They hugged her.

Jonathan reached out for her. She took Jonathan from Gregory and kissed him on the cheek. She held him.

"Thank you all so much for coming, this meant the world to me. How long are you going to be here in Atlanta?" She asked her parents.

"We are leaving Monday morning." Her mother answered.

"I hope you all will come to our house tomorrow. We will have a barbecue."

"That would be great." Her father exclaimed.

"Isaiah will pick you up from the hotel, tomorrow afternoon. Is that ok?" Nicole asked.

"That will be perfect," her mother answered.

"Your sister would be so proud of you." Gregory added.

"Thank you, Gregory. I can't wait to get home and watch the videos of her that you made for me."

"Greg is right. Kyla is smiling down from heaven. Congratulations, you deserve it." William said.

"Thank you, Daddy." Nicole said, hugging him as tears welled in her eyes. "I love you, and I will see you tomorrow." She said to her mother as she hugged and kissed her. She released her mother and faced Gregory. "Thank you for everything. My sister was a lucky woman to have you." She hugged and kissed Gregory on the cheek.

"I was the lucky one." Gregory responded.

She kissed Jonathan goodbye.

Her mother took her grandson from Nicole, so Gregory could help her husband carry the art out to the truck.

"Will Aunty Nicole see you tomorrow?" She asked her nephew.

Jonathan shook his head yes. He was sleepy. "I love you, Aunty Nicole."

"I love you, too." She kissed him on the cheek again.

Her family began to exit the gallery with their art. Nicole saw the drawing of Rashidi still on the tripod.

"Wait a second!" Nicole shouted. She removed the portrait from the tripod and handed the framed portrait to her father. "Please, give this to Yvonne. I promised her that she could have it." Nicole escorted them to the door. "Good night, see you tomorrow."

Peppa and Brian walked up to her. "I am so proud of you." Peppa said. "I knew you could do it."

"Thank you, Momma. It means so much to me, having you here, sharing this special moment with me." She hugged and kissed her. "And you too, Brian, thank you so much."

"I wouldn't have missed it for the world. Congratulations. Your talent is amazing. I brought three prints, and Peppa bought one for me." Brian said happily.

"Thank you. So what are you plans for tonight? Did you guys want to come back to the house?" Nicole asked them.

"Michelle called us a cab. We are going to drop our art off at the hotel, and then were going to hit the streets. Atlanta is known for its nightlife." Peppa answered.

"We're having everyone over the house tomorrow for a barbecue. Please, tell me that you both will come?"

"Of course, we'll be there. Congratulations, baby." Peppa kissed Nicole on the cheek.

"Thank you. I'll see you tomorrow. I can come pick you guys up. Just call me when you're ready." Nicole offered as Michelle approached them.

"Now that everyone is gone, we need to talk with her, Peppa. Do you know that Nicole is actually thinking about working for BB? All the shit BB put her through, can you believe her?" Michelle asked Peppa.

"I'm going to wait outside for the cab." Brian said as he hugged Nicole goodbye. "Nice meeting you, Michelle."

"Same here, Brian. I'll see you at the barbecue, tomorrow."

"What is this about, Nicole? Are you serious? You remember that I threatened BB, to go public with your relationship. Keep in mind that you moved to Atlanta to get away from him. He is an egotistical, abusive, alcoholic, self-centered, maniac. Have you even thought about Isaiah, and how he might feel, about this so-called business arrangement? How would you feel if Isaiah were to go into business with someone he was previously sexually involved with?"

"Thank you, Peppa." Michelle interjected.

"I hear both of you, and you both have valid points. But..." Nicole was interrupted.

"But? There is no but about it." Peppa insisted.

"Listen to me. We will never receive another business opportunity like this. This isn't about me, it's about us. I believe this opportunity is the very reason Isaiah insisted we open the gallery. Isaiah wants me to be successful." Nicole reasoned.

"Remember, you and Isaiah have just recently got back together. I don't believe that this is the type of success that Isaiah was referring to, but you go ahead, and take advantage of this opportunity. Is success worth losing the man you love?" Peppa asked, bluntly.

"Thank you, Peppa." Michelle agreed.

"You're right, it's not worth it. What was I thinking? I guess I was only thinking about the exposure, and the acclaim. I need to apologize to Isaiah."

"Finally, she's come to her senses." Peppa exclaimed as both she and Michelle hug Nicole.

Nicole worried about how Brock would react when she declined his offer. What would he try next? "Thank you both, for helping me make the right decision."

Brian re-entered the gallery. "Peppa, the cab is here."

"I'll see you ladies, tomorrow. What time tomorrow, Nicole?" Brian asked.

"Early afternoon. Just call me when you're ready. I will come and get you. Bye, Momma, thank you. Bye, Brian." They hugged again.

"Good night, Nicole, see you tomorrow." Peppa said.

"You two be safe." Nicole said as Peppa left the gallery with Brian. Nicole locked the gallery door behind them.

"Excuse me? Can I get some help here, please?" Malik said, with his hands full of empty plastic wine glasses.

"Sorry, Pooh-Pooh." Michelle said, as she hugged her husband.

Michelle and Malik threw away the empty plastic glasses in the large, heavy-duty, trash bags. The empty champagne and wine bottles were also discarded.

Nicole printed the receipt tape totals from the register and credit card machine. She walked to her office, unlocked the door and entered it. She retrieved the drop bag that was locked in her bottom desk drawer and walked back into the gallery. She removed the receipt totals, the cash, and the remaining credit card receipts from the register and placed everything into the drop bag.

She put on her coat.

"Thank you, Malik and Michelle, for all your hard work and effort tonight, I couldn't have done it without you." She handed Michelle a small envelope with five hundred dollars in it. Nicole hugged them.

"That's what friends are for." Michelle said.

"You guys ready?" They are standing at the door with large trash bags. "Let me set the alarm, and we can leave." Nicole said.

———

"Thank you for everything, Isaiah. Tonight was beautiful. Congratulations on the gallery. We'll see you tomorrow at the barbecue." William said, as he exited Isaiah's SUV.

"Barbecue?" Isaiah questioned.

"Nicole said we're having a barbecue, tomorrow, at your house."

Whatever, Isaiah thought to himself. "You're welcome Will, see you tomorrow."

"Yes, thank you Isaiah. This has been a wonderful evening. Nice meeting you, Yvonne." Elizabeth said, as Isaiah assisted her out from the SUV.

"Same here, Mrs. Bennett." Yvonne said.

Yvonne was so happy that they were dropping them off. She was truly tired of hearing praises, regarding Nicole. Yvonne felt as if Nicole's parents were acting as though that freak was born an actual biological female.

"Goodnight, Yvonne." William said.

"Goodnight, Mr. Bennett." Yvonne said, masking her irritation.

Gregory was carrying his sleeping son in his arms.

"See you tomorrow, man," Gregory said to Isaiah.

"See you tomorrow." Isaiah helped Mr. Bennett remove the art from the rear of the SUV.

"I will take the baby, and you can help William with the art, so Isaiah can leave." Elizabeth offered.

"Sure, Mom." Gregory replied.

William and Gregory removed the art from the SUV and carried it towards the hotel.

Isaiah closed the back door of his SUV.

"Alright Isaiah, we got it all, see you tomorrow. You both have a great night. We will call you tomorrow." William said.

"Good night, Will." Isaiah closed the back door and climbed into the SUV.

He put his vehicle in drive and pulled out of the hotel's parking lot.

"I'm glad they had a good time. They are actually very nice people. I really wanted my mother to meet them." Isaiah said to Yvonne.

"They purchased a lot of art tonight. They must really love her." Yvonne stated, trying to sound enthusiastic.

"They do, they were so proud of her. Nicole made me so mad tonight." Isaiah instantly realized Yvonne was the last person he should confide in, regarding Nicole.

Yvonne knew this would be the perfect time to put her plan in motion. "I have some good news for you." Yvonne smiled, wickedly.

"And what is that?" He asked.

"You have done quite well for yourself, here in Atlanta. I'm very proud of you. You have a thriving business, a great home, and you're a great father. I have decided to let Rashidi live with you."

"What, are you serious?" He smiled at her.

"Of course, I'm serious, he's a teenager now, and Rashidi needs his father. I've done all I could do for him."

"Thank you, Yvonne that means a lot to me."

"I just have one little, teeny-tiny, itty-bitty, small favor to ask?" Yvonne asked, sweetly.

"What's that?"

"Let's celebrate, a drink together, to toast the future of our son."

"We should have stayed at the hotel where Nicole's parents are staying. I have a better idea; let's go get Rashidi and Nicole. I want them to be a part of the celebration."

"I want this to remain between us; after all we are his parents." Yvonne smiled, innocently. "We have a lot to discuss. Set some ground rules. Like when I get him, and visitation rights."

"Ok, that's cool."

"We can have a drink at the bar, in my hotel." She insisted.

He pulled into the 'E' Hotel and drove into the parking facility. "They have a great bar in here. I brought Nicole here on one of our first dates." Isaiah said.

Yvonne rolled her eyes.

Isaiah thought he saw Yvonne act like she felt some kind a way when he mentioned Nicole, but he decided to brush it off since he was getting Rashidi to live with him. He parked, got out, went around, and opened the door for Yvonne.

"Thank you. You were always such a gentleman. Nicole is very lucky. Oh, Isaiah, please bring my drawing of Rashidi." She reminded him.

"Oh yeah, I almost forgot." He opened the rear of the truck and pulled out the drawing. He activated the alarm.

They started walking towards the hotel.

Isaiah was going to offer her his arm but decided against it. He didn't want Yvonne to get the wrong impression. He held the door open for her as they entered the hotel.

"Let me take my art up to my room. I'll meet you in the bar." Yvonne continued towards the elevators.

Isaiah walked into the bar/nightclub and took a seat at one of the few empty tables. Isaiah looked at his watch; it was 10:08 pm.

Several minutes later, Yvonne approached Isaiah in the bar at the table he selected. "So, what are you drinking, Mr. Mathis? My treat." Yvonne smiled.

Isaiah stood up and held the chair out for Yvonne to

take a seat. "Please, allow me. It's the least I could do, considering how happy you have made me, tonight. What can I get you?"

"I will have a Vodka cranberry. And I know you're going to have a Hennessey and Coke? Am I right?" She smiled.

"Yes," he smiled. "You have a great memory."

She responded a little to exuberantly, "The heart never forgets." Yvonne smiled.

Isaiah ignored her remark.

The waitress approached them.

Isaiah ordered the drinks.

The waitress left with their order.

It was time to execute plan A, Yvonne decided. "Isaiah, I have a confession to make. The gallery opening tonight was not my real reason for wanting to come to Atlanta. I came here to see you. I never truly apologized to you for what I did, while you were locked up."

"I'm good." Isaiah said, embarrassed where the conversation was headed.

"No, please let me finish. I need for you to understand where my head was at. I had lost my entire family, and you, all in the same month. I was due to have the baby at any moment. I had nothing. I was devastated and all alone. I had no one, except me. How was I going to raise a child alone, in that condition? I couldn't even take care of myself. You were sentenced to serve five years, which turned into ten. I didn't know what I was going to do."

"I was incarcerated while trying to provide for my family. You had my mother. She would have helped you."

"Your mother hates me." Yvonne stated.

"So what? My mother knew your circumstances. She would have been there for you. You were carrying her only grandchild."

"I hated asking her for anything."

"What do you mean? You had your own private account. I left you over ten thousand dollars. The rent was paid in advance for a year. Your car was paid for. I gave you everything you wanted. What more did you need?"

"I only wanted you, but I knew I couldn't have you."

"What do you mean, you couldn't have me? I didn't receive a life sentence. You should have waited for me. I did everything for you, and our unborn son."

"I know, and I'm sorry, I made a mistake. I met Derrick in the apartments we lived in. He was our neighbor. He saw the police take you away. The police seized everything. Derrick asked what happened, and I told him the truth. He said he wanted to be there for me, and at that particular point in time, I really needed him. I wouldn't have survived if it weren't for Derrick. I'm sorry; it wasn't supposed to end that way."

"Yvonne, why are you telling me this, now? It's over and I understood. You have a husband and I'm engaged. Life goes on."

"I walked out on him, last month. I couldn't fake it anymore, he wasn't you. Isaiah, I want you back."

Isaiah was speechless. He was stunned by her confession.

The waitress returned with their drinks.

He tipped the waitress generously, and she walked away.

"I love you, Isaiah and I always will. The day you were paroled, I intentionally started an argument with Derrick, so I could leave and come see you. He wouldn't let me leave. For the last three years, I have been begging Derrick to divorce me. I know I made a terrible mistake. Please, forgive me. You belong with me."

"Yvonne, if you would have been standing there, when I got out of prison, I would have taken you back without question. But the way I feel about you now, is not the same. I will never love you the way I did, back then. Too much time has passed. I love Nicole."

Yvonne wanted to scream that she knew the truth about Nicole. She wanted to ask him; how could he be in love with a man? "Isaiah, you don't know how long I've fantasized about making love to you again. What it was going to feel like lying in your arms again, after all these years. I know that you could learn to love me again. If we made love, I'm sure the love you felt for me would return. And if it doesn't, you will never have to see me again. I'm giving you custody of your son. Let's try one more time, for Rashidi."

"I can't do it. I love her, Yvonne. What we had, is in the past. I have no desire to have sex with you. Why can't you be happy for me?"

Because she's a man, Yvonne wanted to scream. She did not want to reveal that she knew Nicole's secret, because Isaiah might be embarrassed, and leave her at the hotel. "You know what, you're right. Please forgive me, for almost ruining a perfect evening."

Yvonne realized that plan A, failed miserably. Honesty is not always the best policy, she thought.

Well-groomed patrons were entering the bar.

She realized that she was going to have to be extra careful in executing plan B. Yvonne began plotting to get him away from the table and up to her room.

"I'm not sure if I told you this, but you did a great job raising our son, while I was locked up." Isaiah smiled at Yvonne, trying to end the conversation on a positive note.

"Well, thank you." She smiled back at him as she touched his hand on the table.

Isaiah wanted to pull his hand away but decided against it.

"It was easy. You gave me a great son."

"Speaking of our son, we need to hurry, so I can pick him up. He is going to be so excited when I tell him the good news."

At that very moment, Isaiah's cell phone began to ring.

Isaiah stood up and excused himself from the table. It was Nicole.

"Hello?" He answered, as he exited the hotel and stood out front. "What's up?" He tried to sound angry.

"Where are you? I really need to talk to you. First, I want to apologize. I don't know what I was thinking. Please, forgive me; I got caught up in the moment. If you don't think I should accept the position, I won't. You were right."

"Good, thank you for seeing my side. I apologize for getting so upset. I should have held my position, instead of getting upset, and walking away. Guess what? Good news."

"What?"

"Yvonne and I are celebrating. She decided to let Rashidi to live with us. How about that?"

"Congratulations, *that* is good news."

"Don't tell Rashidi. We want to surprise him. We are having a drink at Yvonne's hotel in the bar."

"Oh, ok...." Nicole answered with hesitation, not knowing how to react.

While Isaiah was away on his cell phone, Yvonne reached inside her purse, and removed her bottle of prescription medicine. She opened the bottle and removed three tablets of Benzodiazepines, something her doctor prescribed her for anxiety and insomnia. She placed them in her teeth and grabbed Isaiah's drink. She pretended to swallow them; in case someone was watching her. She put Isaiah's drink to her lips, and inconspicuously let the pills fall into his drink. She swirled his drink around and set it on the table. She used her finger to stir the drink, pushing it back to where Isaiah left it.

"So, how much longer are you going to be, Isaiah? I think Rashidi is ready to go home. Why don't we just meet at home?" Nicole said. "Yvonne is staying at the hotel, right?"

"Yes. I should be home within the hour. What is Rashidi doing? How did his night go with the kids?"

"Hold on, I will put him on the phone."

"Wait, don't disturb him. I'm excited to talk to him in person. How did we do tonight?"

"Michelle and I just balanced the drawer. You are not going to believe it. We sold thirteen originals: forty-five framed prints, sixty-eight packaged prints, and eighty-seven greeting cards. I'll tell you the total when you get home."

"Hell, yeah! I told you baby; it was the perfect time. We already built a fan base, by doing all the different art shows, and music festivals. I'm so proud of you. See you in a minute. I love you, Nicole."

"I love you so much, Isaiah. I'm sorry."

"Don't tell me shit. Show me, how sorry you are, when I get home."

"I will, hurry home, please."

"I will pull into the driveway before eleven, I promise."

"Ok."

"Bye, baby." He hung up his cell phone and walked back into the hotel bar.

A sharp dressed man was talking to Yvonne at the table.

Isaiah understood that men would find Yvonne attractive, she is a beautiful woman. He watched her interact with young man, and then Yvonne dismissed the man. He sat down at the table. "I noticed that you didn't give up your digits

"He wasn't my type. He was a little too young for my

taste. Anyway... back to us, we need to make a toast, raise your glass. This is to Isaiah Jerome Mathis, the best father in the world."

They connected glasses.

They both drank their beverages quickly at the same time.

"I should go now. I promised Nicole that I would be home, before eleven."

"Oh, please, just one more."

"Ok, one more. I'll take a beer; I have to drive."

"Ok, I'll go get them."

"I got it." He stood up.

"I want to go; I might get lucky." Yvonne smiled temptingly at Isaiah, as she grabbed her purse.

Yvonne hoped that the drugs would take effect soon. It was just a matter of time. She took her time, making her way to the bar, interacting with every single man she passed.

As soon as Yvonne made it to the bar, the ladies were eyeing Isaiah.

In Atlanta, a single, heterosexual, clean-cut, handsome man, sitting alone in a bar, would not be alone for long.

Isaiah sat at the table enjoying the atmosphere. He was on cloud nine, with the news about his son, and the totals from the gallery, that he started dancing in his chair to the music.

"Hello, how are you? Looks like you're having a good time." She smiled, as she offered her hand.

"Hey, how you doing?" Isaiah flashed his brilliant smile to the attractive young lady as he shook her hand.

Isaiah was becoming more and more relaxed.

"I'm fine, thank you." She smiled.

Isaiah was really enjoying himself, because he hadn't been to a bar alone, in a long time. I got swag, he thought to himself.

"My name is Keisha Brooks, and you are?"

"Isaiah Mathis."

They shook hands politely.

"Is that your girlfriend or wife?" Keisha asked, referring to Yvonne.

"Are you serious?" Isaiah laughed. "If she were either to me, do you think that you and I would be having a conversation?" He laughed again.

"I like what I see. So, to be honest with you, I really don't care who she is."

"Now, Keisha, are you always so, uh, aggressive?"

"Always." Keisha reached for his hand again.

Isaiah pulled his hand back.

"To answer your question, she is the mother of my

son. We are here celebrating because she is granting me custody of my son."

"Congratulations, how old is your son?"

"Rashidi, he's thirteen. Do you have children?" Isaiah asked her. He already knew the answer.

"No sir, I'm aggressive, but I'm not irresponsible." Keisha said.

Isaiah smiled, pleasantly surprised.

"So, please tell me that you are single, Isaiah?"

"Unfortunately, I am not. I have a beautiful, talented fiancé'."

"Yet, you're here, in a bar, on Friday night, with your son's mother, and you're talking to me."

Isaiah was starting to get hot; he suddenly felt odd. He felt sweat forming on his brow. "The operative word here is, *talking*. My wife...fiancé, is an artist, and at her show tonight, I'm sure she did a lot of talking, with all kinds of men. No big deal."

"I should have known; all the good ones are taken. Well, if that doesn't work out for you, please keep me in mind. Here's my card." She handed him her card.

He looked at the card, but the lighting was dim. So, he stood up and placed her card in his wallet. He couldn't wait to show Malik the proof that he could still attract the ladies.

"Thank you. What do you do for a living, Keisha?" He sat back down.

"I am an intern at Grover/Young Hospital, and currently in school to become a pharmacist. What's your occupation?"

"I'm a mechanic, I own Isaiah's Complete Car Care, in Decatur and Norcross; in the process of opening a third location in Riverdale." He stood back up and handed her one of his cards.

"Can I ask you something, Isaiah?"

"Go ahead," he said, wiping off the sweat from his forehead.

"Why is it so difficult to find an unattached man here in Atlanta?"

Yvonne suddenly appeared and set their drinks on the table with her purse.

"Hello, how are you?" Keisha introduced herself to Yvonne, extending her hand. "I'm Keisha Brooks."

"Hello, Keisha," Yvonne said, ignoring her outstretched hand, "it was nice to meet you. I'm sorry, this is a private party."

"Sure, I understand. It was nice meeting you Isaiah, congratulations, with your son."

"Thank you. Good luck to you, tonight," Isaiah winked, as Keisha walked away. Isaiah began to feel dizzy.

The room was swaying to the beat of the music. Isaiah tried to shake it off.

"Isaiah, are you ok?" Yvonne asked, pretending to act concerned.

"I'm good, I need to go. They are waiting for me."

"Can I finish my drink, please? Drink your beer. You want some water?"

"No, sit down, finish your drink. I need to hurry up and get home."

"Ok." She took her seat and a sip of her drink. "You don't look so well. How much did you have to drink at the gallery?" She asked.

"None, I was too busy playing chauffeur today. I haven't eaten since lunch with Rashidi. It's got to be the alcohol on an empty stomach." His symptoms were becoming worse. He was beginning to become alarmed.

"Are you going to be able to drive home? You're making me nervous." Yvonne stood up.

"I just need to sit here a minute." It was hard for Isaiah to talk and say the words he wanted to say.

"Who was that woman? Did you know her?" Yvonne sat back down.

"I just met her here... tonight."

"What did she want?"

"Nothing...we talked."

The pills were obviously taking effect on him,

Yvonne noticed. "Let me go get you a glass of water. You don't look so well. I'll be right back." She snatched her purse from the table and walked away.

By the time Yvonne returned to the table, Isaiah was visibly slumped over.

She and two hotel bellboys assisted Isaiah to his feet and put him in a wheelchair. "Isaiah, can you hear me?" She asked tenderly in front of the bellboys.

"Hey...what's up... what's going on? Where are you taking me?" Isaiah asked groggily.

"I need your cell phone. I need to call Nicole and tell her to meet us here. I'm going to take you up to my room. I can't let you jeopardize your life, by driving in this condition."

"Yes...that's...a good idea. She'll come...and get us." He smiled. "Let me...talk to her."

"Let me get you to the room, first." She instructed.

Eleven

Nicole's cell phone rang, she looked at the number, it displayed unknown.

"Hello," she answered, wondering who would be calling her after 11:00 pm at night.

Rashidi was downstairs playing the video games.

"Is this a bad time? Can you talk?" He asked.

She recognized his voice.

"B.B, why are you calling me so late? What if Isaiah had been home? This would have caused a huge argument."

"Exactly. We need to schedule our first meeting. I want to show you the new location of the sports grill. Just like the old days."

"BB, I can't take the job. I really appreciate the offer and thank you for considering me."

"What do you mean you can't take the job?" He asked.

"For one, I have no intentions of ever having sex with you again."

"That decision is not yours to make."

"Two, I will never have sex with anyone, unless he is my husband, Isaiah Mathis."

"You can't legally marry in the state of Georgia."

"Three, I would appreciate if you would not contact me again."

"You're making a *big mistake*. I would hate for something to happen to your little friend."

"I would hate for something to happen to you." She hung up the phone.

———

"Relax. Just lay back and let me take your shoes off." Yvonne said.

Isaiah was on his back, on the hotel bed, where the bell boys left him.

Yvonne lied to them and told them that Isaiah was her fiancé. She claimed that he had food poisoning from a sushi bar.

Isaiah lay there helplessly, wondering why Yvonne

was lying to them. She reached inside in his slacks and removed his cell phone.

"How do I work this thing?" She asked Isaiah.

"Give... it... here," He sluggishly reached out for his cell phone.

She backed away from the bed.

"I got it. Ok, I found it, here's her number." She turned off the phone and pretended to dial the number.

Isaiah faded in and out of consciousness. He attempted to get up and couldn't.

Yvonne pretended to have a conversation with Nicole. "Hello, Nicole? Nicole? Can you hear me? Yes, how are you? It's me, Yvonne. Yes, he's right here. Don't worry, he's ok. Isaiah must have eaten something that disagreed with him because he can barely walk. Yes, I had to bring him up to my room. I didn't want him to be embarrassed in the bar. He really needs you here. You know what room we are in, right? Yes, 3305. Of course, bring Rashidi, you have to carry Isaiah out of here. You want to talk to him? Sure, hold on." Yvonne held out the phone to Isaiah.

"Just...tell...her...to...come...and...get me." He stammered as his eyes closed.

"Did you hear Isaiah? He said to hurry up and come pick him up. Ok, tell Rashidi, we love him too. Ok, great, see you in a minute. Goodbye." Yvonne set his phone down on the nightstand, next to Isaiah. "Ok, now let's get you out of these clothes. I have fantasized a long time for this day. I never stopped loving you, even when I was married to Derrick. When we were making love, I would fantasize that he was you." Yvonne kissed Isaiah deeply on the mouth. "I need you. We can raise our son as a family. I'm sorry for how I ended us. I promise I will make it up to you. Ooooh, I can't wait to feel you inside of me." Yvonne reached for his belt buckle.

Isaiah grabbed her wrists, firmly. "No." He had difficulty speaking.

"What are you doing? I saw the way you looked at me, when I was dripping wet, in the towel. Do you remember all the times we made love in the shower?"

"No."

"No? What's wrong with you? You don't like real women anymore, Isaiah? I know the truth about your drag queen fiancé,' seeing is believing."

Isaiah opened his eyes and looked at Yvonne. "Did you honestly think I would let my son live with you, and your boyfriend, with his ten-and-a-half-inch dick? Prison was worse than I thought. Do you fuck him, or does he fuck you?"

"Nicole...is...a woman."

"Oh, so he is a woman now? He had a sex change?"

"...Yes."

"Does everyone know that Nicole had a sex-change? What if I called the same news station from the gallery, and made a public announcement? The gallery would be forced to close, one day after the grand opening." Yvonne laughed.

"Everyone associated with Nicole would crash and burn, including Mr. Brock Bass. Is he a faggot, too? Oh my God, does your mother know the truth about Nicole? I wonder how your mother would feel, if she knew her soon to be daughter-in-law, is a female impersonator. Yvonne wouldn't be so bad then, hunh? Isaiah, I recommend that you let go of my wrists, or I am about to make some serious phone calls."

Isaiah reluctantly released his grip on her wrists.

"That's better. I know how to keep a secret. You just have to make me want to." Yvonne unzipped his slacks and fondled his limp penis.

Isaiah tried to tell Yvonne, "No..." Isaiah shut his eyes and the drug induced unconsciousness overcame him forcing him to sleep.

Yvonne kissed him passionately again on the mouth and neck, his penis was becoming erect. "Damn, it's bigger than I remember." She removed his penis from the opening of his boxer shorts. She climbed into the bed, between his legs. She put Isaiah inside her mouth; his penis was rigid as stone. She sucked on him.

Several minutes later, Yvonne pulled his swollen penis out of her throat and mouth. "You like that, don't you?" She said, gasping for air.

She stood up on top of the bed and removed all of her clothing. She sucked Isaiah's dick back into her warm, wet mouth as she felt the thick base of his penis, throb in her hands. She was masturbating simultaneously, savoring each stroke with her mouth and throat. She moaned in ecstasy with Isaiah's huge penis lodged deep in her throat. She achieved orgasm all over her hand, onto the sheets. She pulled Isaiah's dick out of her mouth to catch her breath. She noticed that he was still at full attention, ready for more. Yvonne removed all of Isaiah's clothing.

After she caught her breath, she mounted him. She rode him feverishly once she found her rhythm.

Finally, several orgasms later, Isaiah exploded inside of her.

TWELVE

Knock... Knock...Knock... Someone was knocking on the door.

Yvonne is awakened by the sound of someone's knocking on the door. She looked at her cell phone; it was 4:05 am.

Isaiah is sound asleep, lying behind Yvonne, with his arm around her.

She got out of the bed to answer the hotel room door.

The knocking had become pounding on the hotel room door.

She rushed to the door, and opened it wide, allowing Nicole to get a full view of her naked body. "What are you doing here?" Yvonne pretended to be surprised.

"Is Isaiah here?" Nicole asked, visibly shaking.

"He's asleep." Yvonne smiled as she stood behind the door, allowing Nicole to enter the room. "Please, come in?"

Nicole entered the room.

Yvonne was closing the door, when Michelle jumped out, hidden on the side of the doorway and forced her way in.

"Move, bitch." Michelle said, as she closed the door and locked it.

"Hello, Michelle, how are you?"

Michelle punched Yvonne so hard in the face that saliva flew out of Yvonne's mouth. Yvonne fell to the carpeted floor, holding her face.

Nicole rushed Michelle to prevent her from hitting Yvonne again. "Michelle, please, you promised."

"I told you I didn't like that bitch. Malik, my husband, told me what you said about me." Michelle puffed out her cheeks, mimicking her.

Yvonne got up off the floor with the help of the hotel room wall.

"You're going to jail. I'm calling the police!" Yvonne screamed.

Michelle pushed Nicole out of the way.

"Bitch, if you touch that phone, I'll break your fucking neck." Michelle said, through clenched teeth.

"Sit your bony ass down, right here in front of me, and shut the fuck up."

Yvonne obeyed.

Nicole walked over to bed and saw Isaiah sleeping peacefully.

Under the sheets, it was obvious that he had no clothing on. Tears involuntarily fell from the corners of Nicole's eyes. There are visible lipstick stains on his lips and neck.

Nicole became overwhelmed and walked towards the door.

"What are you doing? Wake his stupid ass up!" Michelle demanded.

"Michelle, I have to leave." Nicole said fighting back tears, reaching for the doorknob.

"I wanna hear what his sorry ass has to say."

"What do you want to hear him say? That he wants a real woman?" Nicole didn't care, anymore. "Michelle, he has obviously made his decision, he wants his son's mother. Please, Michelle, let's go." Nicole opened the door.

Michelle towered over Yvonne, and leaned in, face-to-face. "Bitch, if a cop comes knocking on my door. I want you to know, I will serve life for killing your ratchet ass. Do you understand me, bitch?"

Yvonne nodded in agreement.

Michelle and Nicole walked out of the door.

Yvonne got up off of the bed and locked the room door. She then grabbed the hotel room phone, and dialed 9, for an outside line. She started to dial 911 and decided against it. *How would the police react to unconscious man lying in the bed? Would they want to question to Isaiah? What if they found out what I did to him?* Yvonne pondered all that had transpired in the last few hours.

In the hotel hallway, Nicole collapsed to her knees, and cried openly.

Michelle gently rubbed Nicole's back, trying to console her. "I wouldn't have believed you if I hadn't seen it with my own two eyes. We need to get out of here." Michelle said, she assisted Nicole to her feet and escorted her down the hall.

Michelle reached into her pocket for her cell phone, and speed dialed her husband.

"What's up Babe, did you find them?" Malik answered.

"Malik, your boy is fucking with his baby's momma."

"Isaiah?"

"Hell yeah, Isaiah. That asshole was asleep, buck-naked when we walked in. He didn't even wake up. You need to hurry up and get here. I knocked the shit out of that bitch, and she fell to the floor."

Michelle and Nicole stood waiting for the elevator.

"Baby, no."

"Yes, I did. That bitch answered the door naked, grinning in Nicole's' face like she won the lottery. I told that bitch if she calls the police, I will serve life for killing her stank ass. Are the kids still asleep?"

"Yeah." He answered.

"Don't leave them alone. Bring them. Put them in the truck, under a blanket, they'll be fine."

"You forgot Rashidi is here. Remember? Nicole brought him back when she came to get you. You two hurry up and get the hell out of there."

"I'm trying. They are in room 3305, at the 'E.' Call me when you get here. I love you, Pooh-Pooh."

"I love you, too." Malik hung up the phone.

She placed her cell back into her pocket. "What the hell is taking this elevator so long? You should have let me beat her ass."

Nicole is sobbing uncontrollably.

"Girl, it's alright."

Finally, the elevator arrived, and they stepped in.

Michelle pressed the lobby button, and the doors closed. Michelle couldn't believe the audacity of Isaiah.

She wanted to knock the shit out of Isaiah. I bet you that would have woken his ass up, she thought.

Then the elevator rang, letting them know they had reached the lobby. They exited the elevator towards hotel parking.

"We will wait for Malik in the car."

"Michelle, it's over," Nicole cried.

"You damn right, it's over. You can stay with us, until you figure it out."

Nicole wiped the tears from her eyes.

Michelle decided to change the plan. They made it to the car, and she helped Nicole inside. She jumped in the driver's seat and started the car. She pulled out her cell phone and dialed her husband.

"Hello, Malik, we made it to the car. Have you left already?"

"In a minute."

"Change of plans. I'm going to bring Nicole to the house."

"What? Ok."

"I'm sorry, Pooh-Pooh, we're on the way home. Just stay there, until we figure this out."

"All right, baby."

"Thank you, Pooh-Pooh. See you in a minute."

———

Michelle and Nicole arrived at Michelle's house at 4:55 am.

Nicole was still crying, as Michelle escorted Nicole into her home.

She put Nicole in the den and made her lay down on the couch. She brought her a pillow, blankets, and a box of tissues.

"You want me to turn on the television, Nicole?" Michelle asked.

Nicole shook her head no.

Michelle backed out of the room and closed the door quietly.

Malik was standing in the hallway by the den door. "Let's talk in the bedroom." She whispered.

Her husband followed her into the bedroom. He closed the bedroom door. They sat on the side of the bed.

"So, what the hell is going on?" Malik whispered.

"Hell, I don't know. We walked in the room; he was buck-naked in the bed, sound asleep."

"How you know he was naked?"

"Hell, he had the bed sheets around his waist, with no shirt on. That bitch answered the door naked."

"What the hell? That don't even sound like Isaiah."

"Well, your boy fucked up. That poor girl in the den is devastated. Malik, I wouldn't have believed it, if I hadn't seen it with my own eyes. You should have seen that bitch, prancing around, like she's all that. I knocked the shit out that bitch. She wasn't there for Isaiah when he was locked up. Now, all of a sudden, she wants him back?"

"So, what did Isaiah say, when all the shit was going down?"

"He didn't say anything, he never woke up."

"What? Something ain't right." Malik stood up. "Let me go get Isaiah and see what the hell is going on."

"Where is Rashidi? He shouldn't have to deal with all this drama."

"I put Da'vian at the other end of Malik Juniors bed and put Rashidi in Da'vian's bed."

"What are we going to do about Nicole?" Malik asked.

"She's going to have to stay here for a while."

"Isaiah has obviously lost his mind. I need to hurry up and get to the 'E.'"

"Yes, you do, room 3305, on 14th and Courtland." There was a knock on their bedroom door.

"Come in." Malik said.

Rashidi walked in their bedroom, in his pajamas. "Where is my Dad? I keep calling my parents cell phones, and neither of them are answering. Did something happen?" Rashidi asked.

"Please, come sit right here." Michelle patted the edge of the bed, between her and her husband. "Everything is fine," She hugged Rashidi.

"Yeah, they good. What makes you think something is wrong, man?" Malik asked.

"I heard someone crying. I looked out the door, and saw Nicole crying, running down the stairs." Rashidi answered.

Michelle and Malik immediately jumped off of the bed, and ran into their son's bedroom, down the hall.

They parted the curtains, just in time to see Nicole pull out of their driveway in her car.

THIRTEEN

Isaiah's eyes fluttered open. His was lying on his side. He felt what he thought was Nicole's arms, wrapped around his waist. His head was throbbing with pain, and he felt nauseous. He gently removed the arm from around his waist and sat up on the side of the bed. Where am I, he thought, looking around the hotel room.

"Good Morning, sleepy head," Yvonne said sweetly.

Isaiah jumped up, and backed away from the bed, stumbling against the wall. He suddenly realized that he was naked and snatched the comforter off of the bed to cover his naked body.

"What the fuck is going on?! Where am I?!" Isaiah yelled.

"You're in my hotel room. Remember, we were celebrating last night, because we got back together. You got drunk, and we made love, like it was the first time. And then you passed out."

Isaiah's stomach emptied into his mouth. He covered his mouth and ran towards the open door in the room.

Yvonne heard Isaiah release his stomach contents. "Are you ok?" She spoke loudly. "I told you to slow down on the drinks. You never could handle your alcohol."

Isaiah slammed the door shut.

Yvonne casually got out of bed and put on her bra and panties.

After several minutes, Isaiah emerged from the bathroom, draped in the comforter.

"Where are my clothes?" He asked.

"Exactly where you left them, on the chair, by the desk."

Isaiah grabbed his clothes, and quickly disappeared, back into the bathroom.

She heard him turn on the shower.

She quickly retrieved his cell phone from under her pillow and cut it on. She placed it on the desk.

She continued to get dressed.

After the shower, Isaiah re-entered the room, fully dressed, carrying the comforter. He threw the comforter on the bed. "Where the hell is my phone?" He growled.

"Well, aren't we forgetful this morning? You know it's on the desk."

Isaiah didn't remember anything. He knew nothing except that he was mad at Nicole for contemplating Brock's job offer. Maybe I had sex with Yvonne to get back at Nicole, Isaiah thought. He also remembered that Yvonne was going to let Rashidi live with him. Maybe that's why I had sex with her, he thought. He couldn't remember. His thoughts were jumbled and unclear. He certainly had no intentions of getting back with Yvonne. The very thought of having sex with her, repulsed him.

"So where do we go from here? Should I pack up, and move here? Or are you coming back to Florida, with Rashidi and me?"

"Yvonne, what the hell you are talking about?"

"Let me refresh your memory, Isaiah. Yesterday, I found out the truth about your little boy friend, Nicolas. You know, seeing is believing? I found the manilla envelope in the bottom drawer in the kitchen."

Isaiah froze, speechless.

"I choose to keep that information to myself. Then at the gallery opening, you and the freak had a fight about the football player. By the way, what was that all about? Anyway, on the way back to the hotel, to drop off her parents and me, I decided to give you a bit of good news. I said Rashidi could live with you. So, we started celebrating. You were pissed off at Nicole, and before I knew it, you were drunk, and couldn't keep your hands off of me. You said that you never stopped loving me, and then you said that you wanted me back. Then we came up to my room, and made love until daybreak. Then your drunk-ass passed out." She walked up to Isaiah. "Look at my face. While you were passed out, your fiancée, Wendy Williams, and her best friend, Precious, forced their way into my room."

"Nicole was here? Nicole saw me in bed with you?" Isaiah panicked.

"Precious beat the shit out of me, and now, I'm about to call the police. I am going to make damn sure, that she will never lay a hand on anyone else."

Isaiah grabbed Yvonne by the shoulders. "Did you hear me? Nicole was here, and saw me in bed with you?" Isaiah asked her again.

Yvonne ignored his questions. "So, I ask you again, where do we go from here? Am I moving here? Or are you moving back to Florida? There is no way in hell, I will ever allow my son to live here with you, and that *thing*."

"Where the fuck are my keys? I need to find Nicole." Isaiah asked.

Yvonne hid them under the comforter. "Where do you think you're going? We need to talk about this. Why do you think I came here? To get you back. You belong with me and your son."

Isaiah looked for his keys on the desk, and in the drawers. "My mother was right, you ain't shit. If I lose Nicole because of your bullshit, Yvonne, I will kill you." Isaiah promised.

"Speaking of your mother, how will Gladys react, when I tell her the truth about you, and your future husband? She will fall to her knees and rebuke the both of you. Yvonne won't be so bad then, huh?"

"Leave my mother out of this." Isaiah continued to look for his keys.

"I can't believe this shit. You're in love with a man, now?" Yvonne laughed, crazily. "You know what, how about I tell the police, that Nicole held me down, while Michelle assaulted me? I wonder how much time an accomplice would receive for death threats and assault? How would the police react, when they found out that Nicole was born a he? How can you marry Nicolas, if he's in jail? I have an even better idea. How about I tell the police that you raped and assaulted me, because I didn't want to get back with you, or because I wouldn't let you have custody of my son? Look at me, look at my face. I have proof. You shot your DNA inside of me last night. And guess what? You already have a record of being a violent, convicted felon. If I can't have you, neither can Nicole."

Isaiah pulled all the bedding from off the bed, and heard his keys hit the carpeted floor.

Yvonne quickly picked up the hotel room phone and dialed 9. She dialed 911. "The only way you will ever get your son, is with me. Now, what should I tell the police, Isaiah?"

Isaiah grabbed his keys from off the hotel room carpet. "I don't give a fuck, what you tell the police. Fuck you, Yvonne."

Isaiah stormed out of the hotel room.

"You'll be sorry." Yvonne thought aloud.

About the Author

Sean La'Mont is a California native currently residing in Atlanta, Georgia with her family. Though her writing has appeared in the June 2008 Ebony magazine, this is her debut as a novelist. She is known nationally for her charcoal portrait art. Art lovers are encouraged to visit her websites.

www.seanlamont2010.com
www.glbtqart.com

Also by Sean La'Mont

The Truth Kills

The Truth Revealed

The Final Truth

MBISHIRI- The Journey of

Benjamin

WHIN- What Happened in Nevada

Mr. Charlie!